MW01241783

PULSE

By

D. M. Glass

Pulse

2012 by D. M. Glass through CreateSpace

ISBN 9781477533352

Cover photo by D. M. Glass

Title available through www.amazon.com

For Marie, my constant source of inspiration, encouragement and mad editing skills. This book would not have been possible without your endless support. And a special thank you to my other two favorite editors, Calli and Maria for their encouragement, ideas and brutal honesty.

Chapter 1

"Who should I suck the life from tonight?" Victoria wondered as the last hint of daylight disappeared from the Cleveland skyline and the city streets began to fill with the predictable characters of the urban nightlife. She stepped out of the shadows and sauntered slowly down Columbus Avenue, her long black overcoat blowing behind her. She listened closely to the sounds of the city; horns honking, people yelling, dogs barking, random gunshots, kids laughing, doors slamming, grass growing and clouds racing by. As she walked, her dark brown hair blew in the brisk springtime air and her steel gray eyes took in every sight: the drunken college kids stumbling out onto the street, laughing and hollering; the homeless man with the scraggly beard begging at the street corner; the yuppie couples out on the town with their polished shoes and Gucci attire. She loved this time of night, when the city was just awakening. The lights come on, the thumping music rises from the clubs, and the people emerge from their daily cocoons to become their true selves, selves they keep hidden in their day-to-day life. You can feel the pulse of the city begin to beat faster as the night becomes darker.

She scans the streets as she walks, always aware, always searching; searching for the one that would fulfill her endless hunger. Every night she walks these streets and every night she aches. She knew she should accept her fate and embrace it as so many had, but for her it was a curse brought about her unwillingly. In that lies the irony; although she hated what she was, she was afraid of death. She prayed for it and feared it at the same time. If she could end her endless internal turmoil and still live, she could finally find peace. Until then, she hunts.

As she searched the streets, her mind focused. Blocking out all other distractions, she thought only of the hunger inside. She searched for just the right one and as she walked through the crowds of people, she would gently brush her hand on them. Softly, subtly she touches an arm, a hand, a back, or a midriff as she walks. In each touch she can see. In each touch she can feel. See and feel the joy, the pain, the anger, the peacefulness, the good and the evil in each person. It was not always clear pictures she could see in her mind's eye, sometimes it was scattered images, light and darkness and she could feel the emotion from deep within a person's soul. That is how she found them, the ones; the ones with evil in their soul; in their thoughts, in their actions. Those were the ones that she sought out; those were the ones that gave her a sense of redemption for what she did. They deserved it. They were evil and the world would be a better place without them. If she had to submit to her fate, to what she was, then she would give it a purpose: to free the world of these terrible beings.

As she searched, something pulled her attention to the other side of the street. It could have been the sounds of laughter, it could have been the sight of the three beautiful women, but it was the deep green eyes that fixed her sights; eyes that slowly fixed on hers as well. She stood frozen in the moving crowd absorbed in those eyes. Eyes that stared back, eyes that seemed to see her, see inside her, see through her. It was not just the intenseness and beauty of them that pulled her in; there was something comforting in them, something familiar. She wondered if she knew her as the woman's head turned to keep Victoria's gaze as she continued on with her friends. The mystery woman's long black hair blew softly against her caramel skin as she watched Victoria watching her, urging her with her eyes to come to her as she was being dragged away by her companions. She knew it more than just a simple attraction and she had to go to her. She did not know why, only that she had to.

Victoria was about to cross the street when her concentration was broken by a man who rushed by, bumping into her. Dark images flashed in her brain and an overwhelming sense of dread and death filled her. She refocused on the short man walking swiftly down the street and began to follow him, keeping in the shadows as he turned the corner down a quiet side street. She now saw why he was moving so fast, his eyes darting quickly back and forth through his thin round frames. Up ahead, she saw her, the object of his attention. She had long curly red hair and was wearing a short denim skirt. His prey walked along, her high heel shoes clicking along the sidewalk, completely unaware of the thoughts of rape and murder running through her stalker's mind. It would be so easy for Victoria to stop him now, but she waited and continued to follow him. She had to be sure. Sometimes thoughts did not turn into actions and so she had to be sure before she took him.

The man followed the woman into her apartment building, keeping far enough behind avoiding being seen. Walking up three flights would normally have tired him out, but not at this moment, and his soft-soled shoes gave him that extra quiet bounce in his step. At this moment he was focused on one thing, pleasure; the pleasure of seeing her beg for mercy as he forced himself upon her; the pleasure of her screams as he rammed himself into her harder and harder. It was a pleasure many craved but only a few had the guts to fulfill. He had the guts; the guts and ability to do it. All those other guys talked shit, but he was the one making it happen. He was the one who could take who he wanted, when he wanted. She laughed at him when he approached her in the bar. All he did was ask to buy her a drink. She looked him up and down and then said no thank you but as he walked away he looked back and she was laughing with her friend as they stared at him. Humiliating. She won't be laughing when he was choking the life out of her.

She slipped the key into the lock of her apartment door and flung open the door carelessly. As she closed it, she felt a jarring as the door suddenly stopped. Something was blocking it and as she turned, she saw his face. He had his right foot halfway into her entrance, but before he could take another step, his mouth opened to a silent scream as his eyes filled with fear. The woman never saw what was behind him, but she saw the puddle of blood forming on her doormat. Quickly, the man was being dragged backwards down the hall, kicking his feet trying to gain some footing, his hands outstretched towards her as he grasped for something to grab onto. He disappeared in the stairwell and the woman stood there in shock. By the time she composed herself enough to go to the stairwell, it was empty.

Victoria stayed hidden behind the man as she dragged him down the stairwell and into the dark alley. She set him down on the ground behind a dumpster; her hand still lodged in his back, her fingers wrapped around his spine. She did not have much time so she knelt down beside him and removed her hand from his back. She could smell the blood as it poured from his flesh. He was still gasping as she slowly raised him toward her and placed her mouth over his wound and she could feel the life pouring into her as she sucked the warm blood from his body. Her body quivered with intensity as it filled her, as it fed her. Oh, how wonderful it felt as it swam through her body, filling every void, every vein, bringing with it life-life everlasting, life eternal. These were the moments that all self-loathing was brushed aside as the pure pleasure poured into her, filling her with an overwhelming sense of euphoria that nothing else in the universe could equal. Not even sex. As his heart slowed, she began to relax; a moment of peace in both her body and mind. She sat back against the wall, closed her eyes and sighed.

When she was done, she opened up a nearby sewer grate and tossed his lifeless body down the dark hole. She heard the sounds of splashing water echoing throughout the vast cavern as his corpse hit the sludgy waters of the city's garbage. *Just where he belongs*, she thought as she wiped her mouth and checked herself for spillage, which she knew was unlikely, but one could not be too careful. She took a quick scan of the area and when she felt it was safe, she fled the alley.

She was several blocks away before it hit her: the guilt, and the shame of what she was. She tried to justify it by ridding the world of the evil doers to feed her hunger, but the anguish was still there. Others could feed and feel nothing, but not Victoria. Sure she had to feed, sure she was doing the world a service by saving future victims, but in the end she was a killer. And although she never wanted it, this was her life. She had tried to remove herself from this world several times, but she could never follow through. She was too scared to die, but hated to live in this hellish existence. This was her curse.

And now she had a new problem: who was the woman behind those eyes?

Chapter 2

Sophia was entranced. In a crowd of people, the dark-haired beauty with the steel gray eyes jumped out at her, transfixing her. She gasped as she watched her, her long hair cascading over her strong, yet feminine shoulders and down her back. She seemed oblivious to the cool night wind as it blew her black, full length coat behind her. Although the street was filled with people, it seemed as if she was the only one on the street and she could not look away. Sophia saw her looking back at her too; she could almost feel the intensity in their gaze and if she was not with her friends she may have stopped, something she normally would not do. The trance was broken when the woman suddenly turned away. Sophia scanned the crowd, but she had disappeared. *That was weird*, she thought. She had never experienced a feeling like that before and as she and her friends walked on, those steel gray eyes stayed frozen in her mind.

"What were you looking at?" asked her best friend Paula.

"Nothing," replied Sophia. She would have said something but they would have thought she was exaggerating the whole incident. She was not even sure herself if it really happened the way she saw it because it seemed so dreamlike. It was like those scenes in a movie when everything around the main characters blurs, leaving them the only objects in focus. And as quickly as she appeared, she was gone. It was just her luck the woman ran off. *Figures*, she thought. Even though she tried to shrug it off, Victoria was emblazoned in her mind.

Sophia and her friends were going for their usual Friday night meal together. Paula, her best friend, was the glue that held their group together, always making sure they got together on a regular basis. Paula was the first woman that Sophia had seen working on a construction site other than herself and she took Sophia under her wing. A few years older than Sophia's thirty, Paula had been in the trades for fifteen years and knowing how hard it was to be a woman, let alone a minority, on a job full of men, she was quick to give advice to the new ones on the block. Of course, it was also her way of finding out which ones were straight and which ones were up for grabs, and she was not shy about finding things out. Although her many years in construction may have hardened her stocky form on the outside, it only made her heart softer and at first glance many people misjudged her by her misunderstood frankness. She was highly intelligent and although her demeanor sometimes rubbed people the wrong way, it was her openness and honesty that Sophia loved most about her. They clicked that first day they met and became fast friends.

Maritza, on the other hand, was the complete opposite of Paula; she was a complete girly girl and very shy. Having been friends since their grade school days, Maritza was the only one who stayed close with Sophia as she went through college and her coming out. The fact that Sophia was gay was never an issue to be dealt with for Maritza, who replied with "ok" when Sophia nervously told her. It took Sophia days of internal pep talks to finally come out to her good friend and she was almost disappointed with her simple response. She was always a good sport as Sophia and their other friends dragged her to gay bars and pride parades. She never cared where they went, as long as they were together. Having grown up with two brothers, she loved the bond that her and her 'sisters' shared.

They were on their way to pick up their other friends, Judy and Kelly, a couple they hung out with. Sophia met Kelly in college and for reasons Sophia still did not understand, they continued to be friends. They were completely different in their beliefs and morals; Kelly not having any. She was always getting Sophia into uncomfortable situations, like having her occupying one woman why she went off with another. Sophia always felt sorry for them and did not want to hurt their feelings so she was always hanging behind to comfort them, all the while hating the way Kelly treated these nice, brokenhearted girls. She was about to break ties with her when she got together with Judy, a woman she met at a breast cancer awareness walk that Sophia and the others had dragged her to. She did not really care about the walk, she just did not like to be left out, but you would not have known that from the way she talked to Judy when they met. She was completely enthralled as Judy told her of her lover who she lost to breast cancer and how the walk was her way of honoring her memory. She was very different from the other women Kelly had dated before and the others could see the effect she had on her by the way she treated Judy. Kelly swore she was in love, words she had never uttered before, and six months later they were still together; well, kind of. Judy had been trying to end their relationship for a while without trying to upset her, but Kelly could not let go. Sophia liked Judy a lot, she was a giving person with a loving heart, and she feared that Kelly would crush it like so many before her.

As they neared Judy's walkway, they could already hear the yelling from inside her quaint, red brick bungalow. This was not uncommon, given Kelly's other favorite thing-alcohol. When she drank, she got mean, which has made for many ruined evenings. Deep down, Sophia knew Kelly loved Judy; she just was not really good at emotions, monogamy or relationships in general. The girls walked in the front door to find Judy on the floor and Kelly standing over her, screaming and readying up for another punch. Judy was already bleeding from the nose, but Kelly did not seem to notice or care. Sophia and Paula grabbed Kelly and pulled her out of the front door while Maritza tended to Judy.

"What the hell is wrong with you?" yelled Sophia.

"That bitch. She told me to leave and that we were done," said Kelly, breathing heavily.

"So, this is how you handle it, beating the shit out of her?" asked Paula, angrily.

"I didn't mean for that to happen. She just started talking about how she didn't love me and that I wasn't a good person for her and I started getting really pissed. Next thing I know, she's lying on the floor and you guys are grabbing me."

"I should kick your ass right now!" yelled Paula as she shoved Kelly, causing her to stumble backwards.

"Alright, let's everyone calm down," said Sophia as she slid her petite frame between Paula and Kelly. "More violence is not going to help the situation, although I should let her kick your ass you fucking asshole. You know, maybe if you'd treat her right, she wouldn't have told you to get lost."

"I have to apologize to her," said Kelly as she headed for the door. "I didn't mean to do that to her, I love her." Sophia grabbed her arm tightly and pulled her back, stopping her from going into the house.

"I think you should just stay away from her for a while. I think you should just leave."

Although she really wanted to go in the house, Kelly thought better of it and relaxed. "Okay, maybe you're right." Seeming sincere, Sophia removed her hand from around Kelly's arm but was on alert should she change her mind.

"I am just going to go in and check on her. Stay here. Paula, make sure she doesn't come back in the house," said Sophia as she headed in the house. Sophia looked around at the clusterfuck that was before her; scattered shards of ceramic and glass from a broken lamp, scattered clothes about the floor and the contents of Judy's purse thrown about the living room floor. But what got her the most was the blood on the floor. Her eyes scanned the room again and then she was looking at Judy, who was now sitting on the couch quietly with tear-stained cheeks. "Is she okay?" she asked Maritza who was putting ice on Judy's face.

"I'm fine," said Judy. "Good thing Kelly's all talk and no bite. For a dyke, she sure hits like a girl," she laughed half-heartedly. Sophia sat next to her on the couch and hugged her.

"We should call the police," Sophia said.

"I tried that already," said Maritza with a sigh.

"No, I don't want the police here. I just want her gone." Judy could not even look Sophia in the eye when spoke, knowing Sophia would be disappointed in her. She was embarrassed and the last thing she wanted was more attention and for the neighbors to get more of a show than they already had.

"Well, we'll get her out of here then," said Sophia. "We'll try to talk to her and convince her to leave you alone for good," she said as she gently pushed the hair back from Judy's face. Sophia hated to see her friend like this and struggled to keep her tears back. "I can't believe she did this." Judy just sighed as Sophia gave her a kiss on the forehead. "Where's her keys?" Judy pointed to the top of the microwave on the kitchen counter. "All right, call us if you need anything. You okay to stay?" she said, looking at Maritza, who silently nodded yes, but her eyes pleaded for company. Sophia picked up Kelly's keys, took Judy's house key off the ring and left.

Out on the front lawn, Paula was trying to keep Kelly from coming back inside. Though Paula looked tough, she was not used to wrestling bull dykes full of alcohol and lust. With Sophia now there to help, they wrestled her into her red convertible mustang. She did not know where they were going, but she knew she had to get Kelly out of there. She was going to take her home, but decided against it when Kelly kept yelling that she was going to ride her motorcycle back to Judy's when they dropped her off.

"You can't keep us apart, we love each other," cried Kelly.

"I don't think she loves you too much right now," said Paula, her face getting red with anger the more Kelly spoke. Paula was not a big fan of Kelly's to begin with and only put up with her for Sophia's sake and she hoped this was the end of their friendship. She still did not understand how Sophia could be friends with someone as selfish as her.

Not wanting to take her home, they decided to go to Nickels, a favorite hangout of theirs, until they figured out what to do with her. Of course Kelly gave them the idea since she kept yelling "Nickels" over and over until they finally gave in.

"I got the first round," said Kelly loudly, over the music, as they entered the bar full of ladies. He DJ was setting the background for the women on the dance floor and the women encircling the bar, some scouting potential dates, some just sitting and drinking and some hitting on the bar tender.

"No, you have all the rounds," said Paula as Kelly headed off to the bar in the center of the small club. She turned to Sophia, "maybe coming to the bar and getting her liquored up wasn't the best idea."

"Well, I figured if we came here, it might distract her. If she's sitting home alone, she's thinking about going to Judy's." replied Sophia as she led them to a small table in the corner, away from the DJ booth.

"Maybe you're right," said Paula as Kelly returned with a beer for Sophia, a Jack and coke for herself and a coke for Paula.

"Right about what?" asked Kelly, sitting down like they were just hanging out and she had not just beat up her girlfriend.

"That you're an asshole," said Paula snidely.

"And?" asked Kelly sarcastically. To see Kelly's demeanor at this moment you would have never known that anything had just happened. Sophia and Paula looked at each other in disbelief at the way Kelly could just act so callous. There had to be something wrong with her, they were sure of it, they just could not believe that someone could be this cruel and self-centered. Kelly just laughed and got up from the table and made her way to the tiny dance floor.

As Sophia watched her move across the hard wood floor, she thought what a shame she is such an asshole, because she is so hot. Sophia could not remember how they even became friends; they must have bonded over the alcohol that got them through the endless frat parties in college. Just like any group, she figured, there is always the one person that is an asshole and everyone wonders why they are hanging out with them but continue to put up with their shit, but not after tonight. She will keep her away from Judy for the rest of the evening so she can calm down, and then she is done. One thing Sophia would not put up with is abuse. Not towards her or anyone she cared about.

She had seen her mother beaten by her boyfriend one too many times until her mother finally got the courage to take Sophia, a single suitcase and very little money and flee in the middle of the night while he was working. Sometimes at night, she still wakens to dreams of her mother screaming as the asshole pounded his fists into her back and stomach. It was years ago but she still can remember the rain falling on her head as they ran to the women's shelter, seeking refuge. They appeared on the doorstep, wet, cold, tired, and scared and the kindly gray haired woman at the door welcomed them. She gave them beds to sleep in, warm clothes and a place to stay until her mother could get back on her feet. It was that night, as she watched her mother wince in pain while she gently patted dry the bruises on her body that Sophia vowed to never let that happen to her. And she certainly would not put up with someone hurting her friends. She was too young and weak to help her mother then, but she was not too young and weak to help her friends now.

After about an hour of trying to talk over the music, Paula and Sophia were ready to leave. As they looked around the bar, they realized that Kelly was not around and hoping she had not left, they searched the bar. Sophia had her keys, so unless she hitched a ride, she knew she could not have gone far. Fortunately, the bar was small so it did not take long to find her, although Sophia would rather have not been the one to do so.

She heard moaning as she entered the tiny bathroom. Both of the stall doors were open and as she walked by them, she caught

Kelly in a stall with her hand down some girl's pants, who was moaning and panting as Kelly finger-fucked her.

"Kelly!" yelled Sophia. "What the fuck?! An hour ago, you're in love and now you're fucking some girl in the john?"

"Can this wait, Soph? I think she's about to cum and then she's promised to eat me like I have never been eaten before," she said smiling as she continued to fuck the strange girl.

"You are a fucking asshole! You could at least shut the door!" scowled Sophia as she stormed out of the bathroom. She found Paula and the two left the bar in Kelly's car.

After Sophia left, Kelly continued to fuck the girl until she came in an explosion of thrusting and shaking and then stillness. Kelly was not sure if she should fuck her some more or check her pulse as her body lay lifeless against her. She could not even feel her heartbeat. Slowly the girl raised her head, removed Kelly's hand from her pants, and licked her fingers.

"Mmmmmmm" said the girl in a deep growl. "Almost as good as you're going to taste." As she was undoing Kelly's belt buckle, the bouncer stormed in.

"What the fuck is going on in here?!" the Amazonian woman yelled. "No sex in the bathrooms girls, we aren't running a bathhouse here. You wanna get laid, do it somewhere else. And you," she said to the girl, "I told you I didn't want you in here anymore. All you bring is trouble, get out or I'll throw you out."

"I'd like to see you try," she said under her breath, her black eyes ablaze.

"What did you say?" asked the bouncer angrily.

"Nothing, I'm going," she said as she left the bathroom, Kelly following on her heels. When they got outside the girl started walking away from the bar.

"Hey, where you going?" asked Kelly. "I don't believe we were finished yet."

"Look," she said, turning back to face Kelly, "I really should be going, I'm late for work. But, I'll tell you what. Here's where I'll be tomorrow night." She handed Kelly a card. "Come by and see me and we'll finish what we started."

"You're killing me. I can't believe you're going to leave me hanging like this," said Kelly. She grabbed the girl's hand and put it down her pants, oblivious to anyone that might be on the street with them. She pushed Kelly against the wall, shoving her fingers deep inside her. Kelly felt heat instantly and her body shuddered as the girl moved her fingers inside of her. It felt like an octopus inside her. She looked Kelly in the eye and put her lips close to hers.

"Trust me. You come by tomorrow and I will do things to you that your body can't handle," she whispered in a low gravelly voice that both excited and scared the shit out of her. Kelly was too enraptured to notice that she fell a foot from the air when the girl removed her hand and walked away. She couldn't move as she stood there panting, watching the vixen disappear into the night.

Chapter 3

Sophia was immobile as the dark-haired beauty approached her. The music from the club's speakers was pounding in her head, but it was not the music that was pounding in her chest. Her breathing became faster and faster with each step Victoria took towards her; her steel gray eyes piercing right through her. She came through the crowd as if no one else was there, an aisle of clubbers parting as she walked towards Sophia. As Victoria came near, Sophia felt a sudden sense of warmth. She stopped in front of her, not saying a word, just staring. Slowly, she touched Sophia's soft, caramel colored cheek, sending chills down her spine. She stroked her soft black hair. Sophia wanted to speak, to say something, but she could not find words. Victoria leaned in and whispered softly in her ear,

"Come with me." Sophia could feel the warmth of Victoria's breath on her neck and smell the faint scent of coconut oil and her touch made every hair on Sophia's body stand on end. Victoria took her hand and led her willingly through the crowd.

The music became faint as Victoria led her down a long hallway, but she could still hear the beating of her own heart. She led Sophia through a large set of hand-carved French doors into a large master suite filled with candles. The light from the flickering flames danced off of the dark purple walls and made it appear that the people in the massive wall paintings were moving. It felt like the room was alive. The smell of vanilla was strong in the air, intoxicating Sophia as she was led to the large bed in the center of the room. As Victoria turned to face her, her black, silky dress slipped off of her perfect form, falling to her feet with no effort. Sophia was taken aback by her beautiful, soft, pale skin as the candlelight danced across her naked body. Sophia's heart rate quickened as Victoria began to undress her. She slowly unbuttoned Sophia's blouse, slipped it off of her shoulders and let it fall to the floor. She kissed each shoulder softly as she removed her bra straps and undid the clasp, revealing Sophia's beautiful, small but round breasts. Gently she unbuttoned the fly on her low cut jeans. They slipped from her slim frame easily, and Victoria bent down as she lowered her panties to the ground. She could not stop looking in those deep, steel gray eyes as Victoria lightly brushed her fingertips up Sophia's body as she rose. She entangled her hands in Sophia's hair and grabbed hold tightly, pulling her head back, making her gasp. With her other hand, Victoria lightly ran her long, black fingernails down Sophia's neck, following it with light kisses. She came in closer, pressing her naked body against Sophia's warm skin and then brought her face close to hers. Victoria looked deep into Sophia's eyes, brushing her lips softly over hers, teasing her. Sophia could barely stand the intensity and could not wait any longer. She wrapped her hand around the back of Victoria's neck and brought her lips to hers.

Her body quivered as she felt Victoria's tongue dancing in her mouth. They fell onto the bed entangled in each other's bodies, becoming one. Kissing, touching, and exploring every inch of their flesh until they could wait no longer. Sophia felt Victoria's hand reach for her wetness as she reached for Victoria's. Together they touched each other; teasing, rubbing, sending them both into a frenzy time and time again. Victoria grabbed Sophia's hand and moved her arms over her head and laid her body onto Sophia's. She held Sophia's hands above her head as she slowly rubbed her body onto Sophia's as they kissed; Victoria teasing her slightly and Sophia softly biting Victoria's lips playfully. Victoria slid down Sophia's body until she reached her destination. Oh, how she loved the smell of a woman. She dove in, delving in the taste of her. She danced her tongue lightly over her clitoris, then sucking on it as she felt Sophia's body shake and quiver. Victoria sucked harder and harder as she felt Sophia's pleasure fill her mouth and snake down her throat. Her legs still shaking, her hands quivering, her breath heavy, Sophia grabbed Victoria softly by the hair and led her up to her. Victoria raised her head, revealing her beautiful white breasts and stared into Sophia's deep green eyes again.

"You are so beautiful," Victoria whispered softly. Sophia reached up and pulled Victoria's mouth to hers and Victoria plunged her fingers deep into Sophia. She could feel intense heat as Victoria moved her fingers in and out, slowly, then swiftly, then ramming them in and keeping them there moving them inside her. Suddenly she felt a sharp pain in her neck as Victoria bit into her and her body exploded in a wave of pleasure like she had never experienced before.

In the background, she could suddenly hear music, getting louder and louder. She could hear Melissa Etheridge's voice loudly in her brain, "Come on, come on, over and over, it's such an unusual kiss..." She tried to block it out, to keep this moment, but she could not and Sophia awoke to the sound of her alarm. She opened her eyes and sat up in her wet sheets breathing heavy, her body soaking with sweat, Melissa's voice still blaring loudly, "please let me into your eyes, it's 4:23, I try to hold on as you rise". It took her a moment to realize it was a dream before she reached over and hit the snooze button. She collapsed back onto the bed, still breathing heavy and lied there, staring at the ceiling until her breathing returned to normal. Slowly a smile crossed her lips.

At the same moment, half-way across town, in a dark room, in a large bed, Victoria lay sleeping but her body shook and her pupils moved rapidly back and forth underneath her closed eyelids.

Chapter 4

All day at work, Sophia found it hard to concentrate. Between the late night and the dream, she was more tired than usual and although she loved her job as a carpenter, she found it hard to get out of bed this morning. She knew the woman in her dream was the same woman she saw on the street last night and she made the decision that she had to find her. No one had ever made her feel this intense, this good, this unsettled. *What is wrong with me? I don't even know her. I've never even met her.* She tried to concentrate on the cabinets she was installing inside the Cleveland Museum of Art, but her mind kept wandering back to the dream. What a dream; it felt so real. She could still feel the touch of her fingertips on her body and she swore she could smell the scent of vanilla and coconut when she woke. The vibrating the cordless drill did with every screw she put in took her back to the vibrations she felt with every orgasm her mystery woman gave her. But she was not a complete mystery, she knew her name.

"Victoria," she said aloud to herself. Yes it was a dream, but it felt so real.

"Who's Victoria?" came a man's voice from behind her.

"What?" she asked, startled. She swung around to be sure but she knew the voice belonged to Steve, her coworker and friend.

"You said Victoria. Hot date?" He smiled.

"Hot dream, more like it," said Sophia, snapping back to reality.

"Sounds hot, gimme details," he said excitedly.

"Stevey boy, you couldn't handle the details," Sophia said returning to her work.

"Video?" he pressed.

"Go rent a porno and leave me alone," she said.

"You suck," he said jokingly. "I keep telling you, you just need the right man, that's all."

"Dating men like you is what made me turn to women," she smirked.

"Harsh. I could turn you back to our team if you gave me the chance," he tried.

"Trust me Stevey, I have slept with enough men to know that none of them know how to please a woman. And they sure don't understand us."

"Well, I'll give you that one, we'll never understand you," he said.

This was a familiar conversation between her and Steve. He was always trying to get her to tell him hot lesbian sex stories and she was always disappointing him. At first his comments annoyed her, now they just amuse her and it has become a kind of running joke between the two. She liked that he was not afraid to talk to her about her love life, like most of the guys were and his frankness is what Sophia liked about him and she knew that even though sometimes he acted like a complete jackass, she could trust him not to spread her business all over the job site. For some reason, though, the guys all thought she wanted to hear all their problems and Steve was no different. When he was going through his divorce, Sophia became his confidant and it created a bond between them. She did not usually do that with the guys, she would listen but that was it, but she and Steve clicked and Sophia enjoyed working with him and they often did side jobs together. Although they led completely different lives, they held the same work ethic and the same sick sense of humor and so it made for a seemingly short work day when they could work together.

"Why are you bothering me?" she asked.

"I just came to tell you it's time to wrap up," he said.

"Shit, it's time to go already? What the hell happened to the day?" she asked herself, surprised how fast the day went. Steve, having already put his stuff away, helped her pick up her tools and they headed home for the evening.

Sophia went home, fed her cat, showered and went off to Judy's house to see how she was doing. She stopped and picked up Chinese food, Judy's favorite, to take with her. She was just getting home as Sophia pulled up in her pickup truck.

"Oh, you brought food. You're awesome.," said Judy over-dramatically as they hugged.

"I figured you might want some company," said Sophia. The girls walked into the house arm in arm.

"How is mama doing?" Sophia asked, knowing the answer already but giving Judy a chance to vent on her monthly visit with her overbearing mother.

"Brutal. Today, we just happened to run into Jeff," she said.

"Who's Jeff?"

"The son of one of my dad's old work buddies," she said faking interest. "He is thirty three, works for his uncle's business as an accountant and saves all his money because he still lives with his parents."

"Sounds very promising, does he have a vagina?" asked Sophia.

"That would be the one thing he's missing."

"When is she going to give up trying to marry you off?"

"When I either get married or she dies. She could probably walk in on me having sex with a woman and still be in denial," Judy scoffed.

Judy got both of them a couple diet cokes, silverware and plates and they sat at her small kitchen table and feasted on Kung Pao chicken and egg rolls.

"Are you my babysitter tonight? You guys working in shifts?" asked Judy.

"What are you talking about? There are no shifts; I just came to see how you were doing," lied Sophia. There were shifts, but they were trying not to make it too obvious.

"Well, I'm fine. It's no big deal, but it's the last time I am putting up with her shit. We are done. I don't know why I ever went out with her in the first place; she can be such a bitch. She cheats on me all the time. I guess I didn't care because I was never really that invested in it," said Judy.

"Well, I'm glad you're done with her. We took her to Nickels last night and I caught her fucking some chick in the bathroom. This was after she stood there on your front lawn and told me how much she loved you and how sorry she was. I wanted to kill her, but I just left her there instead."

"How'd she get home?" asked Judy.

"Don't know, don't care," said Sophia as her and Judy laughed. "We picked up Paula's truck and then dropped her car back at her place. I left the keys in the ignition, hopefully someone stole it." She laughed when she said it, but she was not kidding. If she did not live in a rental, Sophia might have driven it through the front door. "Has she tried to call you today?"

"There are eighteen messages on my cell phone, all unanswered. Have you heard from her?"

"As far as I'm concerned she can find someone else to hang out with. I'm done. I still can't believe she hit you."

"Well, I don't know why you are surprised, she has quite a temper," said Judy solemnly.

"Yeah, but to hit you? You'd have to be pretty angry to hit someone you say you love."

"You'd be surprised," Judy half-whispered.

"Whaddya mean?" asked Sophia, "surprised by what?" Avoiding eye contact, Judy said softly, "It's not the first time."

"What?" scowled Sophia in disbelief.

"It's not the first time she's hit me. It's happened before. I brushed it off because I really did love her and really believed she loved me," said Judy guiltily.

"Please tell me you aren't going to take her back," scolded Sophia.

"No, I am not going to take her back. Let's just chalk it up to a six month lapse in judgment and forget it." The words were there, but Sophia was not so sure that Judy would not take her back if she walked in here right now and apologized and by the look in Judy's eyes, she knew she was right. Sophia had to keep these two apart for Judy's sake.

The girls decided to watch a little TV after dinner. It did not take long for Judy to doze off, leaving Sophia to watch Law and Order: SVU by herself. Sophia was trying to figure out how many times she had watched this same episode and wondering why she still could not remember what happens at the end when she felt her cell phone vibrate. She went into the other room to answer it.

"Hello?"

"Hey Soph, thanks for ditching me last night," said Kelly.

"You looked like you were doing just fine for yourself," said Sophia angrily. "Something is really wrong with you."

"Look, I'm sorry, I was just blowing off some steam," apologized Kelly unconvincingly.

"What do you want?"

"What are you doing?" asked Kelly. Sophia did not want to tell her where she was. She did not want to even talk to her, but she would like to get her hands on her and give her a taste of her own medicine. Watching bad ass Mariska always got her fired up for justice.

"Watching SVU," she replied.

"Is it short-haired or long-haired Mariska?" inquired Kelly.

"Shorthaired," smiled Sophia as she glanced at the TV from the other room. It was well agreed upon in her circle that a shorthaired Mariska Hargitay was definitely hotter than longhaired Mariska. Not that she was not attractive with any hairdo, maybe it was that they all thought the shorthaired Mariska had just a little bit of a dyke in her and gave them all hope that even she could jump teams. Paula would disagree, liking her long hair better, but she always did have to be different.

"Well, after you're done creaming your pants, why don't you meet me?" she asked.

"Why?" The last thing Sophia wanted to do was put up with Kelly. But she would like to give her a personal message and she would do anything to keep her from coming over to Judy's house.

"C'mon, meet me. Give me a chance to make up for last night," begged Kelly.

"Alright, where?" Sophia agreed.

"Corner of Frehmeyer and Lesko."

"What's there?"

"Some club called *Pulse*. Ever heard of it?" asked Kelly.

"No. Is it a gay club?" asked Sophia. Sophia did not even know why she asked, because she knew she was already going. Something told her to go; that she had to go.

"I don't know. That chick from last night told me to stop by and I don't want to go by myself."

"Are you fucking kidding me?"

"Look at this way, if I'm there then I'm not at Judy's" taunted Kelly, knowing that would get her to agree. She always did know how to push Sophia's buttons, often getting her to do things she did not want to.

"Alright, I'll meet you there in an hour," Sophia reluctantly agreed and hung up the phone. At least she would not have to talk to her long if she was meeting someone. Unable to take her eyes from those smoldering eyes, she finished watching the show and then left a note for Judy and went to meet Kelly.

Sophia started getting nervous as she turned down Frehmeyer Street, her compact Chevy S-10 bouncing lightly over the narrow, uneven brick road. The area was pretty deserted and had only one dim streetlight, casting strange shadows over the rundown buildings. She would not have even noticed the entrance had she not seen Kelly waiting for her. She parked her truck in a small lot across the street and as she stepped off of the curb, she just avoided getting run over by some maniac speeding down the street on a Harley.

"Did you see that asshole almost hit me?" asked Sophia as she made it safely across the street.

"I think it was a chick. Nothing hotter than a chick on a bike," said Kelly, grinning as she looked after the invisible trail the motorcycle left.

"Thanks for your concern," huffed Sophia.

"Sorry Soph. C'mon, I'll buy you a drink. I think the door is at the bottom of the stairs here."

Kelly pointed to a black metal door at the end of the stairway with PULSE written in small squiggly letters above it. It almost looked like the letters were melting, or maybe dripping, either way it was well hidden and a little scary.

"You sure this place is alright?" asked Sophia, suddenly very nervous.

"I'm sure it's fine," said Kelly as she opened the door. The music pounded as they entered the club. "See, just like any other club." Through the hall you could see the crowds of people; some dancing, some at the bar, some talking, some making out. Kelly handed the bouncer her ID, who handed it back to her without looking at it.

"You sure you're in the right place?" asked the large black bald man with a very deep voice.

"Yes," replied Kelly. "I got this card right here," she said as she showed him the card the girl from last night had given her.

"I wasn't talking to you," he said sternly as he turned his gaze to Sophia.

"She's with me," said Kelly.

"Doesn't matter. This is a private club, you have to be invited," he said.

"She's invited, she's with me. Look…" Sophia could not hear what Kelly was saying to the bouncer, but he let them in. As Sophia passed him, he grabbed her arm.

"You have any trouble, you come to me."

"Okay," said Sophia, confused about his concern for her, trying to pull away from his tight grip.

"I am serious. Any trouble, you call for Derek," he said very seriously and then let go of her.

"Okay, thanks Derek," said Sophia as she hurried away from him. "What was that about?" she asked Kelly.

"Maybe he's got a thing for you. C'mon, let's go get a drink."

They watched the massive crowd as they sipped their drinks and Sophia suddenly felt completely underdressed in her jeans and long-sleeve T-shirt. She could not figure out what kind of club this was, but she felt like she had been here before. As she looked around she realized the reason it looked familiar was it was the same club as the one in her dream. From the bar, the DJ booth to the balcony and down to the tile on the floor, it was exactly the same. The club beats were typical background noise but the crowd was anything but definable; men with men, women with women, men with women, women with women with men, trannies, Goths, yuppies. Apparently anything goes here; it was like Club 54 for the modern age, but with a Goth twist. Although here were a lot of people dressed in all black with pale faces and heavy black eye makeup, you could easily distinguish the true lifestyle Goths from the wannabees. She felt there was something different about this club, however. It was not so much the people and the look that made her feel that way, but the vibe. There was a dark, ominous feeling in the place; dark, but inviting.

"So, are you still pissed?" shouted Kelly over the music.

"Pissed and more pissed since I found out it's not the first time," Sophia shouted back.

"I was wondering if she was going to tell you that. Look, I don't intend to do it. I don't understand what happens to me, I just get so mad. I don't mean to do it. Maybe I need medication," Kelly tried to justify unconvincingly.

"Maybe I just need to kick your ass so you can see what it feels like," said Sophia.

"Is that why you came here, to kick my ass?" asked Kelly.

"Actually, yes, and to tell you to stay away from Judy. She's a good person and she doesn't need your shit. And if you ever touch her or even go near her again, I will personally kick your ass. And you know I can do it," Sophia said seriously, as she looked Kelly straight in the eye. Sophia may be more petit than Kelly, but she knew she was serious by the look on her face and the tone in her voice.

"I get it. I'll back off," said Kelly. "And what about you?"

"Right now, I don't want to be around you. Not after what you did."

"We've been friends longer than you and Judy have been friends and you're going to dump me just like that?" yelled Kelly.

"Maybe when you learn how to treat people with love and respect, then I can be your friend again." Kelly was about to reply when the girl from last night appeared at her side, her eyes seeming to glow under the lights of the club.

"I see you came," she said. She looked Sophia up and down and smiled. "Is she with us?"

"No, not anymore," said Kelly angrily as she grabbed the girl by the hand and dragged her away. Sophia heard the girl say "what a shame" as she looked back at Sophia and smiled as Kelly guided her across the dance floor.

Across the club, in the upstairs balcony, Victoria looked out over the crowd. It is so easy for them, she thought. It is so easy for these young ones to submit to their desires. They think they are invincible but they do not realize how vulnerable they really are. Night after night, her children bring their unsuspecting prey back to the club: degenerates, drug dealers, thieves, rapists and murderers, the worst of the worst. That was her number one rule with any of their kills; they must be evil-hearted because those are the ones that deserve it and the world would be a better place without them. Those are the ones that will not be missed. Those are the ones that must be punished. Of course, like any animal hunters, her children like to play with their prey, luring them here, teasing them, playing sex games with them. Giving themselves pleasure as well as giving the evildoer one last bit of pleasure before taking their life. Many of her children are so young and so sheltered, they have no idea what it is like to be afraid, to have to hide, to worry every day if someone will find out your secret and shove a stake through your heart. People believed in vampires in the olden days and were always on the hunt. Today, people see them as more of a myth, than reality and that was good for them. It was safer for them. Maybe she sheltered them too much, but she did not want them to have to go through the many hells she has endured. She was proud of the life she had created here. They kept to their selves and tried to avoid confrontation with any other vampire groups and so far, things have been pretty pleasant. Victoria tried to stay concentrated on her many businesses and stay out of the drama that usually enveloped many of the vampire clans. When there was an issue, it was usually one of the young ones that caused it. They feel so invincible when they are first turned and if they had a wild streak in them, it always tripled and inevitably they would do something stupid. She could not fault them, for the most part they could not help it. It was all part of the learning process.

As she scanned the crowd, she saw Marianna standing there with two women. She could feel the anger and coldness coming from the one with the spiky hair that Marianna was touching. She could not see the other one's face, but she felt drawn to her for some reason. She watched as the angry girl dragged Marianna away and the other girl walked to the bar. The angry girl had no idea what was in store for her as Marianna was as vicious as she was beautiful. Many of her victims loved the angry, hard sex she gave them. She loved to let them fuck her and then make them come to her for more. She was good at the game; too good and she had no particular sexual preference, she was open to anyone that struck her fancy. She was wild, like her human mother, and Victoria feared that one day she was going to bring trouble onto herself and all of them because of her carelessness. If she was not so loyal, Victoria might have sent her back home long ago. She had a soft spot for her.

She followed the soft, dark haired girl's movements as she got a drink. Her thin, strong hands only accentuated the feminine, almost flirtatious way she leaned into the bar as she spoke to the bartender. Slowly she turned towards the crowd and Victoria gasped as she saw them; those eyes, those deep green eyes. She had to go to her. She had to meet her. She had to touch her. She fled the balcony just as Sophia's eyes drifted up in that direction and Victoria made her way quickly down to the main floor. She watched from afar as Sophia sipped her drink, her soft lips gently touching the straw. She imagined them on her own lips. She loved the way her dark black hair fell in pieces on her soft-skinned face and caressed her neck. She stayed hidden as the woman scanned the crowd.

Sophia watched the dance floor as the song changed and people began lining up on the hard teak wood beneath their feet. *Great, organized dancing*, thought Sophia. She decided it was a good time to refill her drink and turned towards the bar. Being a fan of Muse, she knew the song, *Supermassive Black Hole* but never pictured it as a line dance song. Getting her fresh drink she turned back towards the dance floor and was blown away by the site before her. Having expected a typical line dance, she was surprised at the complexity of movement that was happening before her eyes. It was anything but typical with bodies upon bodies in a swarm of what she could only describe as sex with clothes on. It was like the thriller dance only sexy. She could not look away and felt a little turned on by the intermingling dancing bodies. *Now that's a line dance I can get behind.* It took her a moment after the song was over to come back to reality.

Sophia felt like someone was watching her as she watched the crowd, but when she turned to see if anyone was looking no one was there. As a matter of fact, it suddenly occurred to her, that no one seemed interested in her. When a girl seemed like they were approaching her, they backed off or kept on walking as soon as they got close. She looked at herself up and down, trying to figure out what was wrong with her. *Strange*, she thought, *must be losing it.* She sucked the last bit of liquid from her glass and turned back to the bar to get another drink and was stopped frozen in her tracks.

"Victoria," she said, choking on her words, as she came face to face with the dark-haired beauty from her dreams. She was a vision of darkness with her long black skirt and shawl that only slightly covered her silky red shirt. The top few buttons on her shirt were undone and Sophia could not help wondering if her dreams told the truth of what lied just beneath it. She was holding a drink and offered it to Sophia.

"Another drink for you?" said Victoria in that low, sexy tone. Sophia was stunned and could barely speak.

"Thank you," she said as she took the drink, wrapping both hands around the glass to avoid dropping it from her shaking hands and enveloping Victoria's in the process. Victoria lingered in the hand embrace before she reluctantly, slowly, pulled her long slender hands away. Sophia's head was swimming at the sight of her and they both stood quietly staring at each other, neither of them able to look away. Sophia's heart was pounding and she was finding it difficult to think of anything to say. The silence would have been excruciating but it seemed like time had stopped and the world around them disappeared if even for a moment. Finally, Victoria spoke again.

"Would you like to go somewhere a little quieter?" she asked as she began to back away.

"Yes," replied Sophia, but found herself already following her before the word came out of her mouth.

They entered a large sitting room with couches and tables scattered about with some people talking, some groping each other and others just passed out. There was another bar in the corner where a few people were doing shots; the bartender refilling their tiny glasses before they hit the bar. The bartender never spilled a drop, even as her eyes followed Sophia and Victoria moving slowly across the room. Victoria led her to a secluded corner where several people were hanging out. They were laughing and drinking until the two stunning women approached the table. Victoria just looked at them and without saying a word they scattered like cockroaches when the light comes on, leaving their unfinished cocktails on the table.

"Please sit," she said, pointing to the couch. They sat, eyes transfixed. Sophia could feel her whole body tingling. "I am Victoria."

"I know," gasped Sophia.

"And how do you know my name?" Victoria asked coyly, leaning in just close enough that Sophia could feel her breath as she spoke. She leaned back slightly and tried to regain her composure so she could speak.

"I saw you on the street last night. I know you saw me."

"Yes, I could not take my eyes off of you, but that does not tell me how you know my name." Victoria knew how she knew her name but she wanted her to say it. Sophia hesitated.

"I know this is going to sound weird, but I had a dream about you," she said, embarrassed.

"It does not sound weird at all, it sounds interesting. Tell me about the dream Sophia." She said leaning in again. Sophia could smell the coconut oil on her skin and then it occurred to Sophia that she knew her name also.

"How did you know my name?" Sophia asked.

"Maybe we had the same dream Sophia." Sophia loved the way her name rolled off Victoria's tongue, the way her Italian dialect accentuated every syllable. She was entranced in the way her mouth moved and the way she subtly licked her lips occasionally. Her body shivered and she had the overwhelming urge to jump on Victoria right there. She did not know what was wrong with her, she never felt like this with anyone before. She did not realize that Victoria was feeling the same sensations but was trying to restrain herself. This one was different. Victoria wanted to touch her, to feel her, to make love to her, but she did not want to kill her. Turning the focus, Victoria asked,

"So, what brings you to my club? Who invited you?"

"I came with someone who was invited."

"That angry girl with Marianna?" she asked.

"Yes... You were watching us," Sophia realized.

"Is she your girlfriend?"

"Friends...well, ex friends," replied Sophia.

"If she is no longer your friend, then why did you come? You do not seem like you belong here."

"Would it sound too corny if I said I came looking for you?" asked Sophia. Victoria laughed. *Even her laugh is sexy*, thought Sophia

"It does sound a little corny," then she looked in Sophia's eyes, "but I believe you."

"Is it getting hot in here or is it me?" Sophia laughed nervously. She was so intense.

"Perhaps you need another drink?" Victoria asked.

"How about some water?" Before the sentence was barely out of Sophia's mouth, a buff, young, smoldering young man appeared with a glass of ice water. Although startled a bit, she tried to act unruffled and remarked, "This is an amazing building; great architecture. How old is it?"

"I believe it was built in 1805. Are you interested in architecture Sophia?"

"Maybe," teased Sophia. "Maybe I can come back during the day and get a grand tour?"

"What is wrong with right now?" asked Victoria.

"Don't you have to watch the club?"

"My children will survive without me for a little while," Victoria replied.

"Children? Exactly how many children do you have? Because I know a lot of women who've given birth and they don't have bodies like yours." Victoria usually would not make a slip like that but was finding it hard to focus with Sophia's close proximity.

She hoped Sophia would not read too much into the children remark because she was not sure how to talk her way out of it.

"Well thank you for the complement but just because I have not given birth to them does not mean they are not my children," said Victoria, smiling.

"I was going to say, because you don't look old enough to have children this age."

Victoria leaned closer, smiling, stopping short of kissing her.

"You might be surprised at how old I am." She did not know if it was the way her voice took on a certain raspiness as she said it or if it was the way she looked deep into Sophia's eyes, but every hair on her body was standing on end. She was not sure if it was sexual or fear and maybe it was a little of both, but she was sure she wanted to find out.

"As my cousin always says, it's not how old you are, it's how old you feel," said Sophia.

"Well then, I must be okay because I feel like a twenty year-old. After you," smiled Victoria as she outstretched her arm guiding the way. She watched Sophia walk ahead of her, enjoying the view of her swaying hips.

Sophia took in all the magnificent sites from the old building. It was bigger than she imagined from the outside and there were many passages and rooms within rooms. The original hand-carved beams were still intact and the hand carvings on the moldings and balustrades were magnificent. It was unbelievable to her and she wanted to see everything. Victoria smiled as she watched Sophia, who was like a child with a new toy, caressing every carving, every piece of wood, marveling at the structure.

"You like the building?" asked Victoria.

"It's magnificent. It just amazes me how they did all this with hardly any tools. We have so many tools and devices now to do these things that the true art of woodworking has been lost; for the most part anyway. Just imagine how long it took to do some of this work. It probably took a day just to raise one beam in this place where now we can build a house in a day. It's amazing." Victoria could see the excitement in Sophia's eyes and hear the passion in her voice. To feel that passion again would be wonderful. She remembered feeling that way about painting, but had not even picked up a brush in years. She was almost a little jealous.

"You seem very interested in the fine woodworking, is it a hobby of yours?"

"It's what I do. I'm a carpenter," said Sophia proudly. "I mostly do commercial work, but custom carpentry is where my passion is. I do that as much as I can, but I have to do the other to pay the bills."

"You are quite interesting Sophia."

As they were walking, Sophia saw something out of the corner of her eye. She turned and saw them in all their magnificent glory; before her were the French doors from her dream.

"Just like in my dream." She slowly walked towards them and took in their splendor as she ran her fingers over the carvings. She felt the cut marks, the rough sanded edges, and the amazing texture of the two hundred year old wood.

"I love seeing this through your eyes, Sophia. Sometimes when we are surrounded by something so long, you forget how beautiful it is."

"No one could ever forget how beautiful you are," said Sophia as Victoria joined her at her side.

"It has been quite a while since someone has been around long enough to forget," Victoria said solemnly.

"I don't see how anyone could ever leave you."

"Forever is a long time Sophia. It is hard for someone so young to understand."

"Sometimes forever isn't long enough," said Sophia as she stared deep in those gray eyes.

Victoria knew she was in dangerous territory and needed to take a step back. She was afraid if she touched Sophia, she could not let her go. She was not like the others; there was definitely something different, almost familiar about her.

"Can we go inside?" asked Sophia.

"I am not sure that is such a good idea."

"I didn't dream about this for nothing. I have to see the inside", Sophia pleaded.

"If you go inside, there is no turning back Sophia."

"I couldn't turn back now if I wanted to. Open the doors Victoria," she said sternly.

Sophia's eyes opened wide as the doors opened. Exactly like her dream, candles burned everywhere, surrounding the big beautiful bed, where just hours ago she dreamed they had made love. Maybe it was just a dream, but it did not feel that way. It felt real and she wanted it again. She wanted to feel that fire again. Sophia walked inside and turned to Victoria who was still standing in the doorway and held out her hand. Victoria was afraid to touch her, for she knew the moment she did everything would change. The fantasy was more than she could hope for and if she touched her and felt evil she would have to kill her and she could not bear the thought. She did not want to know but Sophia's eyes were pleading.

"Victoria, please." Reluctantly, but unable to control herself, Victoria stepped in and took Sophia's hand. Instantly she felt flashes of light. She felt unbelievable warmth and goodness and an overpowering sense of innocence and passion. She pulled away. She could not do it; she could not take her innocence.

"You have to go!" she said, frightened of the intense emotions that were overtaking her.

"What's wrong?" asked a stunned Sophia.

"Nothing," Victoria stuttered. "I cannot do this."

"Cannot do what?" asked a stunned Sophia.

"Touch you," she said, her voice trembling. Priding herself on keeping her composure, she hated the way she was falling apart. She did not understand why she was so nervous, as she had been around beautiful women many times before. There was something more than a simple attraction to Sophia and she was not sure she could handle it.

"Why, do I repulse you that much that you can't even imagine the thought of touching me?" asked Sophia.

"Oooh Sophia, you have no idea how much you do not repulse me. I would love nothing more than to hold you and kiss you and make love to you right now, but I cannot," she said trying to avoid her gaze.

"If you want me so bad, what's the problem?" Sophia asked urgently.

"You are so good Sophia. You are so innocent. You have no idea what I am and what I can do to you. You should go now before it is too late." Sophia came closer to Victoria, who quivered as Sophia's hand touched her face, bringing it close to hers.

"I'm a big girl Victoria and can take care of myself and I don't want to go," said Sophia and placed her lips onto Victoria's. They both lingered in the moment as the magnetic force that joined them raced through their bodies, both of them feeling the intense rush of heat and passion that connected them. Sophia felt like she was going to have an orgasm just from the kiss when the moment was broken by Victoria, who grabbed her shoulders and pushed her away while still gripping them tight. She seemed to look right through Sophia.

"I cannot give you what you want," Victoria said through clenched teeth.

"I'm not asking for anything but tonight," said Sophia, knowing it was a lie as it was coming out of her mouth. She did not understand how Victoria could push her away when she knew she felt it too.

"With you, Sophia, it could never be just one night. You have to go," she said as she released her. Sophia came closer.

"I won't go."

"Then I will," said Victoria as she fled the room.

Sophia ran after her but lost her in the winding passageways. She felt like she had been running in circles for quite a while and stopped, breathing heavy, her head spinning, not understanding what the hell just happened. Things were getting fuzzy and she needed some air. She continued swiftly up and down the halls until she found the entrance to the club. She pushed her way through the crowd of people on the dance floor, past Derek and out of the front door. She felt dizzy, like the world was spinning and she could not focus. Suddenly, Derek grabbed her and was sitting her down on the sidewalk and putting her head between her legs.

"Breathe. Breathe slow." He kept her head down until her breathing began to return to normal. She looked up at Derek's face with pleading eyes.

"Victoria, where's Victoria?" she asked between breaths.

"She's gone and you should be too," he replied.

"Why do you keep saying that? Why doesn't anyone think I belong here? It's just a club."

"It's not just a club and Victoria's not just a woman," said Derek as he helped her up.

"I'll give you that one Derek; she's definitely more than a woman."

"Trust me. Go home and forget about this place and forget about Victoria," he said as he led her to a waiting black Sedan. He put her in the car and told the driver to take her home and before she could even refuse, he was speeding her away.

Chapter 5

Sophia was exhausted. Her company was working on a new addition to the art museum and it was getting close to the finish deadline so they were working seven days a week, ten hours a day. The money was nice and she was sleeping well, but she was too tired to do much else. The one thing she was doing plenty of was dreaming.

Victoria filled her nights with passion and lust. Every morning she awoke in a pool of sweat; of course the wetness between her legs was not sweat. Sometimes they were not even having sex in the dreams, just talking and holding each other, but the intense feeling was still there. The dreams seemed so real that she was always surprised to find herself alone in her room when the alarm went off. In her dreams, she could smell the candles and the scent of Victoria's skin. Everything seemed so real, down to the coolness of Victoria's skin and the sound of her heart pounding as they held each other. In many of her dreams, they were in exotic locations like on an emerald field overlooking a vast body of water or in the middle of the woods under a waterfall, places she had never been.

She had gone back to the club a couple of times right after Victoria fled from her but had no luck in seeing her. Derek would not even let her enter the club and kept telling her Victoria wasn't there and he encouraged Sophia should just forget about her. Being too tired from working so much and afraid of being rebuffed if she did see her, she stopped going to the club. At least in her dreams she was not being sent away. So for now, the anticipation of the dreams was getting her through the long days but the dreams were not helping her forget about Victoria. She just wished she get her out of her head.

Sophia and Steve spent the day installing new handrails throughout the new addition. It was a tedious process, having to cut and fit every turn, of which there were many. This was the work that Sophia loved the most, the stuff that took time and patience to get it right, to get it perfect. Everyone that walked through the museum would run their hands along their work of art and it had to be perfectly smooth. She could get lost in every detail and before she realized it an entire day would be gone. This kind of work made the days go fast and as she walked out of the door at the end of the day, she could not believe it was already getting dark.

She slowed as they walked out of the construction site and neared the street; Victoria was leaning against the bed of her truck, looking both extremely sexy but completely vulnerable. Steve nudged her arm.

"You know that chick?" he asked.

"Yeah, I know her, and no she won't be interested in you."

"Does she work here?" he asked.

"No, why?"

"I've seen her here after work almost every day for the past few weeks, so I just figured she worked here. Maybe she's stalking you. Watch out for those ones, they're crazy, I know from experience," he said.

"I'll remember that," she said, thinking it was probably him doing the stalking. She said goodbye to him as they got closer, her tone giving him the hint to take off. Although her dreams felt so real, she had not seen her since that night at the club and was not quite sure how to act. She was still pissed off and a little confused. *But man does she look good*, thought Sophia. She was wearing a dark purple satin button down shirt, with a black skirt. She had a long thin black shawl opened at the front and her clothes seemed to be flowing, even though the evening air was still. Sophia's heart nearly stopped as she got closer but she tried to keep her composure.

Sophia was trying to play it cool but she could feel the electricity coming from Victoria. She wanted to grab her and kiss her, but stopped herself. Not only did she not want to seem too eager but they were in the middle of a parking lot. She looked over and saw Steve two cars over looking at her smiling. Luckily, Victoria had her back to him as he held his fingers up in a v and stuck his tongue through them. Sophia flipped him off and he laughed as he got in his car.

"I'm surprised to see you here," Sophia commented nonchalantly as she opened her door and set her lunchbox behind her front seat. She closed the door and leaned against it.

"I am surprised by my presence also; it seems I am unable to get you out of my head. I have been debating whether or not I should contact you," Victoria said while looking away, trying to avoid Sophia's gaze. Sophia lightly chuckled.

"I hear you've been stalking me. You know, you could be arrested for that."

"Are you going to have me arrested?" Victoria asked coyly.

"I think it would be better," said Sophia moving closer and purposefully locking eyes with Victoria, "if I handled the matter myself. What do you think?" Victoria was unable to look away.

"I am at your mercy. What do you plan to do with me?" Victoria asked. Sophia smiled and tilted her head.

"I have a few ideas." She paused, lost in her eyes. "You know, Derek said I should stay away from you."

"Derek can be...protective," said Victoria. "Maybe Derek is right."

"I think maybe he is jealous. I think he wants you."

"Derek in no way fancies me; but he is loyal. He is a good protector and someone I can trust. He knows I care for you and therefore is protective of you also," replied Victoria.

"It's nice to know," sighed Sophia, "that you care for me. I thought maybe it was all in my head after that night at the club. I thought I dreamed that also."

"It is all real. Even the dreams are real to me."

"So, you're dreaming about me too?" asked Sophia.

"I do not know what is a dream and what is reality; it is all so vivid," Victoria replied almost teary-eyed. "I can feel you inside of my soul." Sophia did not know how to reply. Part of her was frightened by Victoria's intensity while another part understood completely because she felt it also. She could not explain it but she felt connected to her, like they were two parts of a whole.

Victoria used every ounce of control she had to break her gaze and move away from Sophia. She looked at the building with awe.

"Would you like to go inside, I would love to take a walk through the museum with you."

"Sure, we can cut through the construction area if you don't mind a little dust. I wouldn't want you to get dirty," challenged Sophia.

"Dirt is my friend Sophia," said Victoria smiling "shall we?"

"We shall." Sophia found Victoria's speech intoxicating. She never knew anyone who spoke so formally. Not only were the words captivating but the tone in her voice and the way in which she spoke drew her in. It was soft, sensual, yet strong with an Italian accent.

The smell of sawdust hit them immediately as they walked in the door. Victoria could not help noticing the way Sophia paused and took in a big breath, like she wanted to soak in that fragrance completely. Sophia showed Victoria around, pointing out all the beautiful wood trim and millwork she had been working on. Sophia stopped as they came upon a staircase. She placed her hand on the bare wood of the handrail and slowly caressed it. She took Victoria's hand and placed it on the handrail where two pieces of wood met.

"Do you feel that? How smooth the joint is?" she asked as she guided her hand along the handrail. "I love the way freshly sanded wood feels. I love the smoothness and I love that even though the wood is hard, the raw surface feels so soft. It's not just the feel of it but knowing that I did that. I made that perfect piece that thousands of people will be using for years to come." Sophia bent down and took a big sniff of the wood. "And the smell, oooh, I love that smell." Victoria was enthralled at how sensual Sophia's love of her work sounded. She intertwined her fingers with Sophia's and pulled her hand close to her face.

"I have always admired people who could make things with their hands," she said while caressing the back of Sophia's hand and wrist with her free hand. Sophia's heart was pounding.

"I'm pretty good with my hands," boasted Sophia.

"I bet you are," she replied as they locked eyes. They stood there for several moments before Victoria finally looked away. "Shall we go see the rest of the museum?" *Damn*, thought Sophia. It seemed like whenever they had a moment and Sophia was ready to move in, Victoria was pushing away from her.

"Sure, if you insist," said Sophia glumly.

"Come, I want to show you the museum through my eyes. I promise, you will not be disappointed," said Victoria leading Sophia through a doorway by her hand.

They appeared in the open part of the museum in a room full of impressionists' paintings. Victoria walked Sophia around telling her about the artists and what each painting was about and why they painted it. She did not care much for impressionists work but she did love hearing Victoria speak about it. She knew so much and spoke of each one like she was in the room when the artist was painting it and knew everything they were feeling.

Sophia's interest did peak when they entered the medieval room; this was her favorite; this was a room she could feel. She wished she could touch the armors and the weapons on display; their craftsmanship was sublime. The intricate details and hand carvings on many of the pieces amazed her. Victoria could look at a piece and tell you a story about it without looking at the information listed. She made each piece come alive for Sophia with her elaborate tales of jousts and swordfights over power and lust. She told of the artisans who created the pieces and how they made them. It was fascinating for Sophia. She had been here a few times but never really appreciated the entire museum, but now seeing it through Victoria's eyes, it became a whole new place. Her stories and passion made it an adventure for Sophia; an exciting place. Victoria never let go of her hand until they left that room and entered a back hallway.

"You sure know your way around here," noticed Sophia.

"I have been here many times; it is one of my favorite places. I get lost in the history here," she paused as if choosing her words carefully. "I feel at home here." They came upon a man guarding a door. Victoria nodded to him.

"Good evening Benjamin," she addressed him.

"Miss Victoria," he nodded back. "I hope you are well this evening," he said as he gave a suspicious glance at Sophia.

"Very well, thank you," Victoria assured him. "Is the room available?"

"For you, always," he said as he opened the door. Sophia nodded and said thank you as they walked in the room. "If you need anything, please do not hesitate to ask."

"Thank you Benjamin, I think we will be fine," replied Victoria and with that he left the room, closing the door behind him.

The room was filled with miscellaneous paintings and sculptures. It seemed to be more of a storage area than a viewing room; some paintings were wrapped in paper and leaning against one another on the walls while some were hanging sparsely throughout the room.

"I know you come here a lot but how exactly do you get access to an obviously private room?" asked Sophia.

"I donate a lot of money to the museum. Money may not buy happiness but it does buy many privileges." Victoria walked around the room, looking at the pieces that were on display. "Some of these are pieces they rotate to the viewing areas and some are just items they do not want to part with and some they store for private owners."

"You being one of the latter, I assume," said Sophia.

"Yes, I own a few." Victoria showed Sophia around the room, sharing stories of who owned the pieces and who created them.

They came upon an oil painting that Victoria owned of a woman lying in a bed. One hand was above her head and the other laying just below her breast. Her hair was disheveled and she seemed delirious. She was completely nude, but it seemed more erotic than pornographic. Victoria stopped in front of it and Sophia came up behind her and whispered in her ear.

"Tell me about this one," she whispered softly. Victoria could feel Sophia's breath on her neck and she shivered.

"It was painted in 1883 in southern France by a then unknown artist, Francois Bouciet," said Victoria. "He liked to paint women, although he tended to fancy spending time with gentlemen more. He uses heavy strokes and loved to experiment with colors." She felt Sophia's hands come around her waist and forced herself not to turn around and sweep Sophia up in her arms.

"What about the woman? She kind of looks like you...tell me about her," Sophia said softly as her hands slowly and softly slid down and then up Victoria's thighs.

"What do you want to know?" quivered Victoria.

"Why did he paint her? Were they lovers?" Sophia's hands moved up and she cupped Victoria's breasts and slowly began to rub them. Victoria was finding it difficult to focus and knew she should stop Sophia, yet found herself unable to resist.

"They were not lovers, but they did sleep together once," she said softly.

"Before or after he painted her?"

"Before," gasped Victoria as she felt Sophia's fingertips delicately caressing her nipples through her shirt.

"Tell me," Sophia said huskily into Victoria's ear and she began undoing the buttons on her blouse. Victoria began telling the story as Sophia's hands caressed her now naked breasts.

"He was already nude when she came in. He said that was how he always worked, that clothes restrained his creativity. He had a perfectly chiseled body and long black hair. His eyes were a piercing blue. As he began to undress her, she could see that he was getting excited. He apologized and said that usually did not happen around women but he felt a connection with her." Victoria paused as she felt one of Sophia's hands slide up under her skirt. Sophia teased Victoria's nipples with one hand and lightly began to rub between her legs with the other. Victoria gathered her voice and continued.

"He lowered the top of her dress from her shoulders and kissed her breasts. I would have stopped him but it felt so good. He cupped them in his hands and his tongued teased my nipples. I was overwhelmed with lust. He told me he had not been with a woman since his youth and wanted to taste me and all I could mutter was 'yes'. He picked me up with his slender, muscular arms and I wrapped my legs around his waist and ravished his hard mouth as he carried me to his bedroom and threw me down on the bed. He quickly pulled my off my dress and buried his head between my legs." At that moment Sophia slipped her hand under Victoria's panties and she could feel Victoria's legs go slightly limp for a moment. Victoria had stopped talking and was now moaning as Sophia slowly rubbed between her legs.

"Did he get you off?" asked Sophia as she pleasured her. It had not escaped her attention that her point of view changed as if Victoria was the one in the story.

"Although he was more prone to gentlemen, he definitely knew how to give pleasure to a woman. My body shook uncontrollably as he brought me to climax," she said with heavy breaths. "And just as I was about to explode he entered me." At the moment she uttered the words, Sophia grabbed her tight to her and jammed several fingers up inside of Victoria. She felt a gush of liquid as she held her hand inside her and moved her fingers.

"Did you like it?" asked Sophia as she began to move her fingers in and out of Victoria.

Gasping, Victoria continued. "Very much so. I was not used to a man, but his shaven body was smooth and I could feel his long hair gently caressing my skin as he thrusted inside of me. He held me tight to him as he brought himself in and out of me, pushing harder and harder with each motion. I felt myself draw blood as I dug my nails into his back when I came again. He then let himself finish and he collapsed beside me and we-they lied together panting for what seemed like an eternity. After a while he got up, grabbed his canvass and paints and began painting her. She is not delirious in the painting; she is simply exhausted from her recent passion."

With those last words, Victoria spun to face Sophia and enveloped her mouth in hers. Sophia grabbed Victoria by the back of her hair and slammed her back against the painting. She pulled Victoria's head back and sunk her mouth onto her neck. Biting and sucking her neck, Sophia twisted Victoria's clitoris between her fingers and felt another gush as her body shook. Sophia could feel Victoria's long fingernails on her back through her shirt and Victoria screamed as she jammed her fingers inside her again. Sophia thrusted them in and out, in and out, until she felt Victoria's hand on her own, holding it there. Neither moved until she felt Victoria's body slowly collapse into her arms and her breathing slowed.

"Let's get out of here," Sophia whispered anxiously in Victoria's ear. Victoria kissed her and the two ran from the room. It felt like they were flying as they raced down the long winding halls and out of the back door to Sophia's truck. Sophia sped home, finding it difficult to watch the road as Victoria kissed her neck and ear and caressed her the entire way there.

They couldn't get in the door fast enough and barely made it to the bedroom before tearing off each other's clothes.

"I have to take a shower," said Sophia, "I'm sure I smell."

"You smell wonderful," said Victoria as she pinned her to the bed and sat herself on Sophia's lower area. She sighed as she looked down at her. She slowly slid her body down onto Sophia's and sank into her nakedness. She held her tight and whispered, "I feel like I can't get close enough to you, I want to crawl inside your skin." Their legs intertwined and fell in between each other's thighs and Victoria slowly began to grind against Sophia. Her body quivered and she stopped for a moment as she suddenly became overwhelmed with emotion.

"What's wrong?" asked Sophia as she brushed Victoria's soft hair from her face.

"I don't know. This just feels so....beautiful," she answered softly. Sophia pulled Victoria closer and kissed her. Their bodies intertwined, fitting together perfectly and both could feel the electricity between them as they writhed together on the bed. She felt Victoria bite her shoulder as their bodies shook together, which only intensified Sophia's orgasm. Sophia smiled as Victoria whispered, "I want to taste you" in her ear. Victoria slid down Sophia's wet body snakelike until she reached her wet paradise. She could feel Victoria's tongue doing things she'd never felt before. Her body shook uncontrollably as Victoria's tongue and teeth danced over her clitoris; not biting but gently nibbling. She then dived inside her with her tongue. Sophia swore she could feel it deep inside her and she grabbed the bedpost tightly and raised her hips as she exploded in ecstasy. After the storm subsided Victoria nestled herself next to Sophia and gently ran her fingers over her body.

Sophia gently caressed the side of Victoria's face and pulled her mouth to hers. She loved the feel of her smooth skin. It was unusually smooth with no imperfections, like expensive silk stretched to the breaking point. They lay there for hours; kissing, caressing and pleasuring each other until Sophia fell off to sleep. Victoria lay with her head on Sophia's chest listening to each breath. She could hear the chambers and valves in her heart opening and closing, pumping blood throughout her body. *What a sweet sound,* she thought. She could feel her fangs coming out with every swoosh she heard. *Oh, how I would love to taste her blood.* As her eyes darted across Sophia's body, she noticed puncture marks on Sophia's shoulder; she was not even aware she had bitten her. She gently leaned over Sophia and lapped up the trickle of blood that was seeping from the wound. She couldn't stop herself from sucking as she felt a rush when the blood ran down her throat and she could see Sophia's life flash through her mind. It took all her energy to pull her mouth away and, slowing her quick breathing, she tried to regain her control. She opened a small wound in her own wrist and let a few drops of blood fall into the wounds on Sophia's neck. The blood, entering the human cells, quickly regenerated the tissue, closing the wounds. She pulled herself away and rose from the bed.

Victoria sat in the chair next to the bed holding her legs close to her and crying. Thoughts were flooding her mind; *what am I doing? What if I could not stop? I do not want to hurt her. I have to control myself. Maybe I could just tell her. Maybe she would not care. Sure she wouldn't. There are usually two responses when you tell someone; either they want to kill you or they want you to turn them. As much as I would want to spend eternity with her, I could not give her this curse. I just have to be more careful. I must feed before I see her. If I cannot control myself than I cannot be with her and that is not an option any more. I can do this. I love her too much to stay away.*

Suddenly she was aware of the approaching dawn as her internal warning system brought her back to reality. She did not need to see a clock or even look outside; it was ingrained in them, like their thirst for blood. Contrary to myth, they could be seen in the day, as long as it was a gray sky and they took precautions. Like medicine for mortals, vampire scientists had created lotions and intravenous medications that could protect them for several hours. Nor would they instantaneously explode. They would first weaken, and then faint and then their skin would slowly burn off. The burning pain would awaken them, allowing them to seek refuge. Victoria was not prepared, however, and therefore knew she must go. She gently kissed Sophia on the forehead, careful not to wake her and left.

Sophia thought she had been dreaming again when she awoke to the alarm and found Victoria was not there.

"You've got to be fucking kidding me. There is no way I was dreaming this time," she said to no one in particular. She leaned over to shut off the alarm and saw a note on the nightstand.

No, it was not a dream.

Sorry, I had to go and did not want to wake you.

I will see you soon.

Forever yours,

Victoria

Sophia sighed as the reality of it all set in. She noticed Victoria's shawl lying across the bottom of the bed and pulled it to her face. She could smell her on it.

"Ahhh. It wasn't a dream."

You would never have known that Sophia had slept only two hours the night before as she sailed through her morning. She was on an emotional high and could barely contain her excitement as she thought about her amazing night.

"You must have gotten laid last night," said Steve as he brought over a bundle of woodwork and placed it on a couple sawhorses.

"What? Why do say that?" asked Sophia, trying to play it cool.

"One, I haven't seen you smile like that ever; two, the dark circles under your eyes; and three, that chick was too hot not to do her," he said as he counted out the reasons on his fingers.

"First of all, I always have dark circles under my eyes and I would appreciate it if you didn't talk about doing her," Sophia scolded. Slowly though her smile returned and she couldn't help herself, "she is hot though."

"See, I knew it. You can deny it all you want but I know all. C'mon, just one little detail," he pleaded.

"I'm not gonna give you details of my sex like so you can beat off to it later. Get your own sex life," she said.

"I have a sex life, but mine doesn't include hot lesbians," he said as he laughed.

"Whatever," she scolded, "just get back to work."

Chapter 6

"Jacoby," Victoria heard herself mutter as she awoke with a jolt. She lied there, staring up at the ornate ceiling, waiting for the knock on the door. What was he doing here? She had not seen him in years and was not ready to see him now. The issue was not Victoria's lack of love for Jacoby, but her lack of patience with his immaturity and callousness. There was a reason he did not stay long in one place, he was – to put it nicely - an asshole. Then there was the expected knock on the door that echoed throughout room.

"Miss Victoria," said Jonathan, her houseman/bartender/friend, in his exaggerated frilly voice, "there is some guy named Jacoby here. He says he's your brother but I'm not sure I believe him. I have never heard you talking about any brother, but he insists he is. He is fine though, I can take care of him if you like." She was quiet for a moment, deciding what to do. If she ignored him, he would just make a scene and that was the last thing she wanted. She knew she could not ignore him, anyway, he was her brother and against her better intellect she loved him.

"Give me twenty minutes Jonathan and then you can send him down," Victoria said from the other side of the door. Jonathan sauntered down the hall and out to the club where Jacoby was pouring himself a cocktail of tequila and his own blood. Vampires could absorb alcohol only when it was mixed with blood, so they either had to inject it directly into the bloodstream, drink it from an intoxicated person or make a blend of blood and alcohol to drink. Eventually it did dispel itself, preventing them from getting too drunk like humans did, but a lot of them still liked the short high it produced.

"She said you should just sit here with me for a while until she gets herself together," he said coming up close beside him, touching his arm with his. Jacoby just looked at him and jumped over the bar onto a stool. He took a swig of the drink and winced.

"You know what they need to come up with is an alcohol you could drink that doesn't taste like shit."

"I can microwave it for you, that usually helps. We have something better though," said Jonathan as he spun one of the mirrors behind the bar. He opened a door and exposed shelves of jarred blood. "These warmers keep the blood at such a temperature that it stays warm for ten minutes after it's mixed with alcohol." Jonathan took out one of the jars and made Jacoby a drink. He slid it across the bar when he was done and leaned on it, flirtingly. Jacoby just ignored his obvious come-ons and slowly put the glass to his mouth. He smiled as he tasted the warm drink. It slid down his throat, warm and smooth, like fresh blood.

"Now that's a drink. I have definitely been drinking in the wrong places," he said. He motioned for Jonathan to make him another and got up from his stool and walked around, checking out the club, but could feel Jonathan's eyes upon him. Jonathan was admiring his spiky black hair and masculine face that gave him an almost sinister appeal and he smiled as his eyes drifted from his head to his well-defined arms and shoulders to his perfect ass. *What I could do with that ass*, Jonathan thought.

"Think again butt pirate," said Jacoby as he continued his tour.

"Can you-?"

"Yes, I can read your thoughts," smiled Jacoby, "and although I'm flattered, I like women bro."

"Don't knock it 'til you've tried it, bro," said Jonathan sarcastically.

"I have, didn't like it. I like being the only penis in the room."

"Well-," Jonathan, who was about to curse him out, was cut off by the ringing of his cell phone. "Yes, Miss Victoria. I will bring him down." Jonathan showed him the way and left him in a huff at Victoria's door. Jacoby just laughed at Jonathan as he knocked on the door.

"Enter," said Victoria.

"Always so formal sis. Are you ever going to lighten up? This isn't the nineteenth century and we aren't royalty," he said as he burst through the door. "Now, give your little brother a hug, I've missed you," he said as he picked her up in his arms and swung her around.

"I wish I could say the same," said Victoria as she pulled away.

"You're not still mad about your sweet thing I took off with are you? I really didn't think she was that important to you and if it makes you feel any better it didn't last long. She took off with one of the Maderon's as soon as we hit Venice." He said, trying to justify his actions, and then slumped himself down on the sofa, kicking his legs up on the coffee table. Victoria walked over and pushed his legs off the table and sat on the couch opposite him.

"I was not upset about the girl, she was trivial. I was upset about the dead man you left in the basement and the two thousand dollars you stole from the safe," she scathed.

"Alright, I'll give you that. Well, I'm sorry I left the rotting corpse in your basement, I was kind of in a hurry and I can pay you the money back," he said unemotionally. His callous attitude infuriated her. He had not changed at all. His charm worked on some, but Victoria was immune to it. Being from the same maker, they could not read each other's minds but she could read his face and always knew when he was lying.

"I do not care about the money, Jacoby; I would have given it to you if you would have asked. I do care that you stole from me and showed me such disrespect as to leave that man in my house. What if the wrong person would have found him? We do not take lives in our own home for a reason Jacoby. It is not like the old days when you could leave a body anywhere or wash some blood away. They have ways to find blood that has been washed away for years and we cannot take the risk. It will only take one of us in jail for them to discover we exist in reality and not just in their books and movies."

"Maybe they wouldn't care what we are," he said.

"They would care. They would hunt us down and destroy us. They would poke and prod and study us and the ones who did not go along with their wishes would be executed. It is better we stay unknown, a myth they cannot prove," she disagreed.

"Well, it's definitely more fun hiding. If they knew about us they could protect themselves and what fun would that be?"

"Whatever keeps you quiet," she sighed. "So, why are you here, money?"

"Oh sis," he said as he came over and sat next to her and put his arm around her. "I was just passing through on my way to Mexico and thought I would stop and see my big sis. It wasn't easy to find you; I've been looking for a while."

"How did you find me?" she asked.

"I didn't find you. I followed Marianna's thoughts once I got close enough. But I've been all over this country looking for you and personally, I don't know why you like this god forsaken place when there is a whole world to explore."

"It is easy to stay hidden here. I can blend in better in a place where there are so many…" she paused, looking for the right words, "different types of people."

"I don't know why you of all people would want to come back here."

"It's a different place then it was 100 years ago and somehow it is--. Forget it, it does not matter. I like it here."

"Forget what?"

"Nothing, I do not want to go into it with you,"

"You have always been so guarded. You know, you should let yourself have a little fun once in a while," he said nudging her closer. She pulled away and grimaced.

"You need a bath."

"Yeah, I probably do, I was-" he tried to say as he sniffed himself but Victoria cut him off.

"I do not want to know," she said as she arose from the couch and summoned two servant girls. Jacoby walked over to the girls and put his arm around them. He could smell their blood.

"This is what I'm talking about," he smiled.

"Jacoby, these girls are loyal and I would like to keep them," she scolded.

"I know, I know. No corpses, I got it."

To the girls she directed, "get him a bath and a room and if he tries anything you object to, please inform me." She waived them off and closed the door behind them. Victoria knew he was hiding something but did not know what and she would have to find out soon otherwise there would be trouble. Trouble always followed Jacoby; actually Jacoby always brought trouble.

If she had trouble she would have to leave and that was not something she wanted to do. She never thought she would ever come back here when she left a hundred years ago, but somehow it has been comforting. Plus, she was established here and doing well and did not want to have to start over somewhere else because it was not as easy as it used to be to recreate yourself. Sure, there were always people who could help you for the right amount of money but it has become harder and harder for it not to be traced. And now she had another reason, Sophia. It had been a long time since felt this way about anyone. She had done a good job of keeping her emotions in check and she felt like her control was falling apart at an exponential rate. She especially avoided humans. They were supposed to be mere playthings, not companions. But there was something about her that

Victoria was drawn to and she was finding it difficult to resist. She felt whole when they were together, like she had found a part of her that was missing. She was lost in the thought of her when her phone rang.

"Sophia," Victoria breathed into the phone.

"What are you doing? Wanna grab some dinner?" asked Sophia.

"Well, I have already eaten and I have to watch over the club," said Victoria begrudgingly.

"Well, maybe I'll swing by there," she replied.

"Do not come here," Victoria said quickly and then realized how that must have sounded. "It is just that we are expecting a crazy crowd tonight. Maybe I can get away for a little while. How about I meet you later, say around nine o'clock?" Sophia agreed and the two hung up. Victoria did not like Sophia coming here for fear that she might end up in someone else's hands, like Jacoby's. She could make an appearance in the club and then disappear without notice. She knew she should not be doing this but could not help herself. She could not tell her no and just thinking about her was enough to put her on an emotional high. Trying to pull herself from her thoughts, she drug herself to the bathroom to get ready for work.

As she looked over the crowd, she could see that Jacoby had wasted no time finding Marianna; the two had an intense sexual bond. They were not interested in being companions but always had this insatiable lust for one another and could not and did not want to resist it. They were true 'friends with benefits'. *How nice it must be to have no conscience*, Victoria thought. She was unfortunately not one of the lucky ones that lost her guilt when she was turned; if anything it accentuated it. Jacoby used to have a conscience, but she did not think Marianna ever had one. She was sitting at a table with her new plaything, Kelly, hanging on her when Jacoby saw her. He sat down next to Marianna, took her face in his hands and the two began to kiss, while Kelly just stared in disbelief.

"Hello sweetness," he said to Marianna when he finally pulled his lips away.

"When did you get into town?" she purred.

"Today. Up for a ride?"

"Always," she said and kissed him again.

"Hey, did you forget I was here?" Kelly huffed. Marianna did not forget Kelly was there, she just did not care.

"You can join us sweetheart, I bet you taste splendid," said Jacoby licking his lips. Kelly was upset, she thought her and Marianna were together. Love is blind, as they say, and Kelly either did not see the way Marianna treated her or did not want to. Marianna was never 'with' anyone, she only used them until she was bored and then tossed them aside, often times literally. Kelly threw

Jacoby a glance telling him to get lost but instead of leaving he kissed Marianna again while looking at Kelly. She had never been with a man before and certainly did not want to share Marianna with this asshole.

"Well honey," said Marianna as she slid her hand up Kelly's thigh, never taking her eyes from Jacoby, "you can join us or you can leave. As always, it's your choice." She was pissed off but finding it impossible to say no to Marianna, Kelly muttered,

"I'll join you."

"That's what I thought," said Marianna, smiling.

Victoria watched as they got up from the table. Marianna grabbed both of their hands and led them out of the club area and back to her room. *At least Marianna is with him,* she thought, she will keep him under control; well, at least she will keep him occupied. She knew that Marianna had been feeding from the girl but she was discreet and the girl was not leaving the complex. She could read her thoughts and knew there was no threat from the girl because of her attraction to Marianna. Many of the vampires had playthings that they kept. Some mortals were drawn to a certain vampire and became theirs while others wanted to become a vampire and therefore would go to anyone who fancied them with the hope that one day they would be given the 'gift', as the mortals called it. Some gift. They would let the vampires feed off of them and the vampires would fulfill their desires, whether sexual or material.

Victoria had had a few playthings over the years but she preferred a long term companionship; therefore she always nested with vampires. Her last longtime lover, who she had been with for nearly sixty years, was killed by a jealous vampire. Devastated by the loss, she had sworn off love and not been with anyone serious since; until now. And Sophia was no plaything. The thing that scared Victoria most about her attraction to this woman was that she knew there would have to be an end to the relationship. It could maybe last a few years, but eventually Sophia would wonder why Victoria was not aging. Unfortunately, Victoria felt she was already in too deep and could not stop and did not know how she was going to end it when the time came. Her only other option would be to turn her and that was something she did not want to do. She glanced at the clock above the bar and saw it was 8:45. She told Derek she was leaving and raced to the coffee shop near Sophia's apartment. Victoria suggested the coffee shop, knowing if they were alone it would only lead to one thing.

Sophia was reading a book and drinking a latte when Victoria arrived. She closed her book when Victoria sat down across from her, not wanting to waste one moment of her presence.

"You like horror novels?" asked Victoria as she took the Stephen King novel from Sophia hands. Their hands touched slightly as Victoria grabbed the book and sent shivers through both of them.

"I love them," said Sophia.

"What do you like about them? They're so gruesome."

"I don't know," said Sophia, "I've always been drawn to them. I guess because it's so far from me. I love the suspense and with a horror novel or movie you never know what's coming next because it's not based in reality. It's usually a surprise and if it can make me jump out of my seat, all the better."

"I just do not understand the wanting to be scared," said a confused Victoria.

"It's the feeling of anticipation. Like when you are watching a scary movie and you know something is coming but you don't know what. You're heart starts racing, your hands are clammy, and you're on the edge of your seat and no matter how much you prepare yourself it always gets you when it happens. It's the thrill," said Sophia excitedly.

"It's a thrill to be terrified that someone is going to get killed?"

"It's only a thrill because you know it's not real. If it was real, it wouldn't give you the same feeling, it would paralyze you instead," explained Sophia. Victoria just sat there with a confused look on her face. She had seen enough real horror to not want to watch it on camera. "The feeling is almost the same as the anticipation of sex. You see this person you are so attracted to, you get tongue tied, your hands start sweating, you heart is pounding and you're never sure what's going to happen. Is this person going to reject you? Are they into you? You never know until that moment."

"Now, I understand that feeling," said Victoria smiling.

"The thing that turns most people away is the gore. That doesn't bother me; watching the surgery channel, now that grosses me out, because it's real."

"It is fascinating to hear you explain this. I have never really watched them. Do you have a favorite genre of horror?" asked Victoria.

"Vampire stories are my favorite, especially the movies." Victoria tried to not let her surprise show.

"Why, do you want to be a vampire?" she asked half joking.

"I think what I love about the vampire genre is the sensualness of them. There are a few exceptions, but for the most part vampire stories tend to be about passion and everlasting love and loyalty. It doesn't hurt that the movies always have hot looking vampires that just ooze sex. A perfect example is Coppola's version of Bram Stoker's Dracula. It's gruesome and scary and most of all it's one of the most sensual movies I have ever seen." Sophia stopped and looked into Victoria's confused face.

"I have never seen this movie," said Victoria. "I stay away from vampire movies because they are usually ridiculous."

"It's not about whether it's ridiculous or accurate; it's about appreciating the underlying stories and the creativity that goes into it. You'll have to watch that movie with me and you will see what I mean. No matter what kind of movie you like, I defy you not to be turned on by it." Victoria leaned in close as Sophia took a sip of her coffee.

"I do not need a movie to turn me on." Sophia choked on her coffee as Victoria's hand touched her knee.

"Let's get out of here," whispered Sophia. Victoria did not answer right away, she was too enthralled. She was lost in the gleam in her eyes, the sound of her voice, the softness of her lips. She took in a deep breath as to take in Sophia's scent. She tried to ignore the pulsating of her blood and focus on just her.

Sophia was brought out of her daze by a sudden shaking. At first she thought it was an earthquake until she realized that Paula had just shook her shoulder.

"Hey Soph, what's going on?" she asked. "Care if I join you?" Paula introduced herself and sat down before Sophia even had a chance to answer. Victoria leaned over and shook Paula's hand and then relaxed back in her chair.

"I am Victoria; it is wonderful to meet you."

"So who are you?" asked Paula, more matter-of-factly than rudely. That was just her style, to the point.

"I am a friend of Sophia's," she smiled.

"Well, I'm a friend of Sophia's and I don't look at her like that."

"Paula, stop it," said Sophia. "You'll have to excuse her, subtlety isn't her strongpoint."

"I find it refreshing," replied Victoria.

"See, she finds it refreshing," she aimed at Sophia. "So, what do you do for a living?"

"She owns a club," Sophia replied for her while giving Paula a sideways leer.

"Among other things," added Victoria.

"Is it a gay bar?" asked Paula.

"Everyone is welcome at my club, as long as you are invited."

"So, am I invited?"

"That is up to Sophia. She has been there once and I think she will agree when I say it is not for everyone," she said seriously.

"She's got that right. I don't think you would like it, it's very Goth," said Sophia.

"I really must be going," said Victoria as she rose from her chair. Paula's presence made it easier to make an exit. She had to try to keep her distance as much as possible to protect herself…and Sophia.

"No, don't go," said Sophia as she grabbed Victoria's hand and rose to whisper in her ear, "I thought we were going back to my place."

"Don't leave on my account," said Paula.

"No, I have to get back to the club; there are things I must attend to. Paula, it was a pleasure."

"Likewise."

Sophia walked Victoria out of the coffee shop and waited while she hailed a cab. She did not need one but she knew it would look odd to walk thirty-two blocks in the middle of the night. Sophia pleaded with her not to go, but Victoria insisted. Before Victoria got in the cab, she turned to face Sophia who was holding the door for her. She leaned in and kissed her softly on the lips and could feel Sophia's teeth lightly bite her bottom lip. If only she could stay. Reluctantly, she got in the cab, never taking her eyes from Sophia. Sophia mouthed the words "call me" as she watched the cab pull away and then went back into the coffee shop where Paula was still waiting.

"Thanks Paula," said Sophia sarcastically.

"What?" chuckled Paula. "I would have left, you should have said something. Where'd you meet her? She is hot."

"I met her at her club when I met Kelly there to tell her to fuck off. But it was weird because I saw her on the street a few days before, then I had a dream about her and then I get to the club and there she is. Actually, I've been dreaming about her a lot."

"Sex dreams?" asked Paula.

"Of course. Well, not all of them, but most of them. The thing is that they are so vivid that I could swear they are real. I wake up in a sweat and swear I can still smell her in the room. It's bizarre. I've had sex dreams before, but not like these," Sophia wasn't sure if she wanted to tell her the other part but couldn't resist. She looked around, then leaned into to Paula and whispered, "I had sex with her in the art museum. That, I know was real."

"Thanks. I didn't need to know that, now I will be picturing you two doing it at the museum when I go back to work there." Sophia just laughed as she sipped her coffee.

"So, are you going to take me there so I can meet some hot chick?" pleaded Paula.

"First of all, even if I took you there, you'd be too nervous to talk to anyone and second of all, Victoria told me Kelly has been hanging out there a lot. I think she's shacking up with that girl we caught her with at Nickels. I think that girl lives there. Anyway, I don't feel like running into Kelly, but if I do decide to go there again I will call you."

"That's all I'm asking."

Chapter 7

Sophia caught a glimpse of Victoria outside the window of the art museum and went out to meet her so the guys would not see her; they would never let her live it down. They ran off to a deserted corner to be alone and Sophia quickly grabbed Victoria into her arms and kissed her. She could feel Victoria's glorious tongue in her mouth and feel the strength of her hands on her back. Suddenly Sophia heard a loud noise and felt a quake. Reality smacked her in the face as she opened her eyes and saw Steve standing over her.

"Get up," he said.

"Fuck," said Sophia disappointed. "You could've given me five more minutes."

"Must have been a good dream," he said laughing.

"It would have been," she said as sat up on the stack of wood she was laying on and shook herself back to reality. Reluctantly she went back to work.

Victoria had a voicemail from Sophia when she woke. She listened closely as Sophia told her of her dream at lunch and how real it was. It was real for Victoria also as she had shared the dream with her. Sophia said she did not have to work the weekend and wanted to see if she was up for a weekend getaway.

"Call me when you get this," Sophia's voice seemed to jump through the phone into her soul. "I miss you." She closed the phone and laid it on her chest. A weekend would be difficult to do on short notice, but would be nice to get away for a couple of days with Sophia. Her thoughts were interrupted by the house phone.

"Yes," she said into the phone.

"Hey sis," said Jacoby, "are you gonna sleep all night?"

"What do you want Jacoby?" she asked annoyed. He might be a problem if she went away for the weekend.

"Well, Marianna has informed me of a carnival down on the lakefront at Edgewater Park and we were wondering if you would like to join us for some hunting." Victoria thought for a moment. It had been a week since she had a good meal and she was not feeling her usual powerful self and she should go and keep an eye on Jacoby. After that phone call, she was on a sexual high and a little release would do her good by bringing her back down to earth. Real feeding, as they called it, cleared the head and released many pent up frustrations. Carnivals were also good places to find all sorts of damned souls that were looking for trouble. Carnivals always attracted some of the worst people so they made excellent hunting grounds and the lake made for a perfect dumping ground.

"Actually, that sounds like a good idea. I still have to shower so give me a few minutes. I'll have Jonathan call and get the boat ready," Victoria said.

"Awesome," said Jacoby smiling. He knew she could not resist a good hunt, no vampire could, even Victoria and her moral high horse.

She was so excited about the hunt that she almost forgot about calling Sophia. She knew she better call her or she might come to the club looking for her.

"I was hoping you'd call. Whaddya think about my idea?" asked Sophia excitedly.

"Well, as much as I would love to run off and escape with you this weekend, it is not going to be possible. How about we postpone it so I can plan for my absence?" said Victoria.

"I guess so," Sophia sounded disappointed. "I guess that's the cost of being a big business woman."

"Sometimes it is difficult being me," said Victoria coyly.

"Did you just make a joke? I don't think I've ever heard you make a joke before," said Sophia.

"Well, there is a first time for everything. How about if I plan us a nice getaway for later in the month? I have a cabin in Hocking Hills we can go to. It has a lake, a fireplace and a hot tub. How does that sound?" Victoria thought it would be easier later in the month with autumn approaching, which brings with it shorter days and longer nights. Her cabin was on a small lake and was well hidden deep in the woods where she owned fifty acres. They would be well secluded from anyone and the trees would provide much shade. Although very disappointed, Sophia agreed.

"Allright. I guess I'll call you tomorrow," she sighed.

"I look forward to it," Victoria said as she bid adieu and placed the phone back in its cradle.

The lights from the carnival danced on the lake waters as they floated across Lake Erie to the waterfront. The lights seemed especially bright against the dark sky and the stars shone brightly on this clear night. The lights from the carnival rides moved in time and a blur followed the Ferris wheel lights as they spun in the darkness. Victoria and Marianna stood at the front of the boat looking out at the swarm of people as Jacoby steered them into a dock position. Victoria put her nose to the air and took in a deep nasal breath.

"Do you smell that Marianna?"

"The smell of fresh blood," said Marianna as a smile slowly appeared on her face. Jacoby docked the boat and the three disembarked.

"We will meet back here in an hour and take them out on the lake together. And Jacoby-"

"I know; no innocents," he finished before she had the chance.

"Be careful and happy hunting," she said coldly as her eyes seemed to glow as the thirst came over her and the three disbanded in different directions.

Meanwhile, Sophia, along with Paula, Maritza and Judy decided to start their evening at the carnival also. Paula, of course, was telling the others about Victoria and how hot she was.

"Are you hiding her from us?" asked Maritza.

"I'm not hiding her. She is just kind of private. Plus she works a lot of nights so she sleeps late in the day," said Sophia.

"Maybe she's a vampire," growled Paula jokingly. "She does own a Goth bar."

"Whatever," said Sophia playfully pushing Paula. "Let's get something to eat."

Victoria was trying to keep a mental lock on Jacoby as she floated through the crowd but was finding it more and more difficult as she could not concentrate on him and locate her prey. She gently touched everyone as she passed them by. The loud carnival sounds echoed in the background but could not cover up the sound of the pumping blood of everyone around her. Everywhere she looked she saw bulging veins and could hear the swishing of heart ventricles opening and closing. Suddenly her hand involuntarily clutched down on someone's arm as violent images flashed through her head. A young girl under him, a raging woman in the background, he hits her, beats her. The young girl is screaming. She looks up at the man, whose arm she was holding. If she had not seen so many different types of horrible people in her lifetime, she would have been shocked by his clean cut appearance. He smiled at her as she took a moment to compose herself. Then she smiled back.

"I am sorry for grabbing you, I thought I was going to fall," she said in her sexiest voice as her grasp on his arm turned to a caress.

"That's no problem, I am happy to help." Oh, this was too easy, Victoria thought to herself. Men were usually her choice for prey because the cocky ones always thought every woman wanted them and it was easy to get them alone.

The girls were a good distance away sharing a funnel cake when Paula spotted Victoria talking with the man.

"Hey, isn't that your chick?" asked Paula, pointing her out to Sophia. Sophia looked and saw Victoria standing there with a man in a suit. At first Sophia thought they were just talking until she noticed the way Victoria was caressing the man's arm. She watched Victoria as she laughed, leaning into him every time, clearly flirting. "What's up with that? I thought she was into chicks," asked Paula. So did Sophia. She did not reply, she just watched as Victoria took the guys hand and led him through the crowd, losing sight of them as they walked behind the merry-go-round. Judy put her arm around Sophia.

"Maybe she's just doing business with him. You know how guys are; a little flattery goes along way."

"Yeah, maybe," Sophia said unconvincingly to her friends and herself. Flattery is one thing, but it looked like more than that when Victoria whispered in his ear and she could have sworn Victoria looked right at her before whisking him away. Sophia knew she had no right to be mad, they had not made a commitment to each other, but it still hurt. She thought they were beyond that; that they were bound. Even as she thought it, she could not believe how she sounded like such a lesbian cliché. You know the one: date one, dinner, date two, moving van. They had not known each other that long and she was mad at herself for letting herself get so attached so quickly, but she knew it was real. It was different than anything she had ever experienced before. She could not explain it but she felt like she had known her forever. She stopped looking in the crowd after her and just wanted to leave. She needed a drink. "Let's get out of here," she said to her friends, who did not argue and whisked her away.

Jacoby and Marianna were already on the boat when Victoria arrived. Jacoby had picked up a slightly chunky girl with bleach blond hair and way too much makeup, who was clearly intoxicated. She was hanging all over Jacoby, trying to undo his pants in front of everyone. Marianna had picked up a young guy who had this crazy, disheveled red hair and a crazed look in his eyes. At first glance she thought he was high on something but quickly realized it was just his craziness showing through. She knew there was no such thing as the devil, but there was such thing as evil and it protruded from every pore in this boy's soul. The man with Victoria looked disappointed when he saw the others on board and Victoria quickly steered his direction to her.

"Ever driven a boat before?" she asked.

"Sure, I can drive a boat." She knew he was lying even before he finished his sentence.

"C'mon," she said as she led him to the wheel. She subtly helped him drive the boat out onto the water. She had him stop the boat when she felt they were a safe distance from shore and at this point she was kissing his neck. She spun him toward her and slipped his jacket off, careful to keep the others on the boat deck below them hidden from his view.

Marianna had moved to the back of the boat and had the boy stripped naked and lying on some cushions on the deck. She was straddling his pale-skinned body with her blouse open, the light from the moon bouncing off her exposed milky white breasts. The boy got so excited that he came on himself. Embarrassed, he became angry.

Marianna grabbed his wrists and held him down as he was about to reach up and grab her by the throat.

"Typical," she mocked him.

"Get off me bitch, I'll show you typical. I'll fuck you so hard you'll be sore for a week," he said angrily. He struggled beneath her to free himself but was no match for her strength.

"I would not let that little pasty thing inside me if you paid me, you pussy-assed mother fucker," she sneered as her fangs protruded. Horror filled his cold eyes as he realized what was happening. He screamed like a little girl as she lunged at him, sinking her fangs deep into his neck.

Jacoby, on the other hand, had no problem putting his penis anywhere and was on the other end with his conquest naked from the waist down and bent over the side of the boat. His perfect naked body glowed as he moved in and out of her roughly. Just as he was about to cum, he grabbed her by the hair, pulling her towards him, and buried his teeth deep into her flesh. He shivered as the blood trickled down his throat and he relieved himself inside of her. He felt her body go limp and pulled away from her. He did not even bother zipping up his fly before he dumped her body overboard.

Victoria had no intention of getting that close with her prey as she loosened his tie and removed it from his neck. She could not stop thinking about Sophia as she unbuttoned his shirt and began to kiss his neck as his arms enveloped her. She hoped Sophia had not seen her, but knew that was just wishful thinking. She had felt Sophia's eyes lock on hers and knew she saw her. She would have to tell her something. The excitement of the hunt had now disappeared and she just wanted to get out of here so she did not waste any more time playing with her dinner. She slid one arm behind his back and one up towards his neck. He could feel the tightening as his breathing became impaired while she squeezed his neck.

"You like raping and beating little girls?" she snarled as she began to crush him.

"Who are-?" he tried to say but her hold on him impaired his speech. "Now it is your turn to suffer." She did not give him a chance to say anything else as she sank her teeth into his neck. She liked to let her prey know why they were chosen. She liked the look of shock and horror in their eyes when they realized their sins had caught up with them. The high she got from their realization that they were no longer in control was almost as good as the feeling she got when the blood flowed down her throat. Almost.

Chapter 8

Sophia could not hear the knocking over the stereo. She was lying on the floor in her pajamas, the haunting sound of Kelly Clarkson's *Irvine* surrounding her,

> *Are you there?*
> *Are you watching me?*

She was staring out her sliding balcony door but seeing nothing. She looked up at Paula, who was standing over her with her keys in hand.

"Have you been lying here all day?" asked Paula loudly.

"No. Only since I stopped throwing up," said Sophia groggily.

"That's what you get for drinking so much." Paula was still talking loud as the song ended and switched to Anna Nalick's *2 am.* Sophia slowly rolled onto her back, exposing her dark circled eyes and her carpet imprinted face.

"What time is it?" she asked.

"What?" Paula asked, unable to hear her over the music. She walked over to the stereo to turn it down.

"What time is it?" Sophia repeated.

"It's 6:30. What are you listening to? These songs are depressing." Paula stopped the CD and took it out of the player. It was a generic CD with the letters STSYWB written on it. Holding up the CD, she asked Sophia, "What's this mean?"

"Songs to slit your wrist by," replied Sophia as she rolled back over on her side.

"Nice," Paula remarked sarcastically as she sat down on the couch. "So it did bother you last night. Have you even talked to her? Maybe it was nothing. Maybe she's a closet case and was just hanging on him so no one would know. Maybe he's gay and they were just hanging out." Paula was trying to rationalize things for Sophia, who was clearly upset about what she saw but did not seem to be getting through to her. She noticed the message light on Sophia's cell phone flashing and picked it up to check the messages. "What's your code?"

"One two three four" Sophia replied softly. The first one was from Judy seeing if she wanted to get lunch, the second from herself and the third was from Victoria.

"Victoria called and wants you to call her," Paula told her. Sophia sat up and leaned back against the couch, pulling her knees towards her.

"What are you doing here?"

"You were supposed to meet me at the movie theater. I called you when you didn't show up and I got worried since you didn't call me back. I'm glad I had keys or you might still be lying here tomorrow morning," explained Paula. Sophia just glared at her. "Have you eaten anything today?"

"Food sounds good." Looking down on her puke stained shirt, she grimaced. "I think I need a shower."

"I'd say so," agreed Paula. She helped Sophia off the floor and she stumbled into the bathroom to shower.

At dinner, Sophia slowly ate her plain, breaded chicken sandwich like she was savoring it. When Paula suggested dinner, she was not thinking Wendy's, but Sophia had insisted.

"You know, I was thinking steak, not burger for dinner," said Paula. "We could have at least gone to a restaurant for a real burger."

"This is my hangover food," said Sophia.

"I think your hangover ended hours ago, this is just depression." Sophia could not argue, she was feeling depressed. She knew she was overreacting but could not help it. This was all new to her; no one had ever made her so jealous before. She prided herself on keeping a clear head and being a rational thinker and she hated this feeling of overwhelming emotion. She made fun of her friends who got so caught up in someone after only a short time and now here she was doing the exact same thing and it scared her. Is this what real love felt like?

"Maybe we should go to the club and see her," suggested Paula. Sophia just looked at her. She knew what Paula was up to, she just wanted to go to the club and was using her misery against her. She knew Sophia too well and was not surprised at all when she agreed to go.

Victoria was in her office amidst a pile of paperwork thinking about Sophia when she got a text message from Derek. *Sophia's here.* Her excitement at the thought of seeing her was clouded by the lie she knew she would have to tell her. She left the safety of her office and as she stepped out onto the balcony of the club, she saw Sophia and Paula at the bar. They were chatting with Jonathan as he fetched drinks for them. Victoria wished she had not brought Paula here; this would make it more difficult. She called over one of her girls and whispered in her ear as they looked upon the two.

"Can you occupy her friend for me for a while?" Jocelyn agreed and made her way downstairs to the bar. Jocelyn had not been talking to the girls for thirty seconds before Jacoby spotted Sophia and made his way to her. *Damn it Jacoby,* thought Victoria as she hurried to Sophia's side. He only had to see the way the two looked at each other to get the hint.

"Sorry, didn't know she was yours sis," he said. Sophia was not sure how to take that statement; he talked like she was a possession.

"Sophia, this is my brother Jacoby," Victoria said. He kissed her hand like an old-fashioned gentleman and said it was a pleasure to meet her. He winked at Victoria and slid away, looking for another unsuspecting human.

"I wish you would have told me you were coming," Victoria said.

"I bet you do," said Sophia angrily. "Do you have another date here?"

"No Sophia, you are the only person I am seeing," said Victoria softly. She was right; Sophia had seen her last night and was now upset. Although she felt horrible about the hurt she saw in her eyes, Victoria could not deny that she felt a little bit of happiness at Sophia's apparent jealousy. "Let us go somewhere more private to talk."

"I don't want to leave Paula alone." Sophia knew Victoria could see right through her as Paula was now in deep conversation with some girl. She was trying, unsuccessfully to play hard to get. Victoria, seeing right through her, took her arm and led her back to her room.

Victoria barely had the doors closed behind them when Sophia blurted out, "I saw you at the carnival with that guy last night." Victoria had an entire story planned out to tell her but as she stood here looking in her eyes she found it impossible to lie to her. Sophia was irritated by Victoria's silence. "Well? Is it a boyfriend? You aren't married, are you?"

"I am not married Sophia and it was not a boyfriend," said Victoria.

"Don't tell me it was business, because you two looked awful cozy."

"A girl's gotta eat," said Victoria playfully. Victoria quickly realized by the look on Sophia's face that joking was not a good idea. She walked towards Sophia who backed away.

"What the hell does that mean? Did you fuck him?" Sophia now had tears streaming down her face and Victoria was helpless to resist. She grabbed Sophia by her arms and looked directly into her eyes.

"Look Sophia, sometimes I have to do unpleasant things in my business but believe me when I tell you this; I did not sleep with him or anyone else for that matter." She wiped the tears from Sophia's face and sighed. "Ooohh.... Sophia. Do you not know that I am completely and utterly in love with you?" Sophia could not speak. She was lost in Victoria's eyes, her touch, her voice, the sound of her breath. Victoria's voice quivered, "No one has ever captured my soul the way you have. A minute does not go by that I am not thinking about you. Rest does not come without dreams of you. When we are apart, my whole body aches for you. When we are together, I want to envelope every part of you within me. And although my head knows that I should not be with you, my heart is unable to resist you. I would die for you Sophia." She kissed Victoria hard on the lips and the two encircled each other in their arms. Sophia did not even feel her feet leave the floor as Victoria lifter her across the room and onto the bed.

Slowly, they undressed each other. For hours they kissed and caressed each other's naked bodies. Sophia's skin was electrified as Victoria kissed and nibbled on every part of her. Victoria could not hold back as Sophia's hands played her body like an instrument. Their bodies exploded as they pleasured each other over and over again until they lay, out of breath and energy, their legs and arms intertwined so you could not tell who was who if not for their contrasting skin tones.

Sophia awoke in a dreamy haze, but as her head cleared she realized it was not a dream this time. She was still here and Victoria was sound asleep next to her. Even under the thick blankets, Sophia could feel the coolness of Victoria's pale skin. She snuggled closely to her and lied there for a few moments hoping that Victoria would wake up but she seemed to be dead to the world, her breathing heavy. After a while, Sophia became restless and decided to go find the kitchen and get some coffee. She dressed and wandered out into the hall, not sure which way to go. As she roamed around the building looking for the kitchen, she reached in her pants pocket to answer her vibrating phone. It was Paula. "Where are you?"

"I'm at Victoria's. Where are you?"

"I'm still here too. Meet me by the club door," said Paula. They each walked around lost until they finally met at the club door. "This place is huge; I've been lost for like a half an hour."

"Don't they have a kitchen in this place? I need some coffee. Hey, sorry about leaving you alone last night," said Sophia.

"Don't be. I met this hot chick."

"Did you sleep with her?" asked Sophia.

"No, we just talked all night. She's got a huge collection of first edition books, you should see the library," said Paula excitedly. Paula was a huge reader so it was no surprise she would be awed by someone who shared her passion. The girls jumped as the door opened next to them and Jonathan appeared, looking especially gay in his sequined tank top, complete with a laughing Dolly Parton on the front.

"Good morning ladies," he said smiling.

"You scared the hell out of us," said Paula.

"How about some coffee?" he asked. The girls nodded and followed Jonathan through the club through another door on the other side. They walked into a huge gourmet kitchen, with dark cabinets and stainless steel, commercial appliances. The ceilings were at least twelve feet high with two huge skylights on each side of the gable roof. It was excruciatingly bright, which explained why Jonathan was wearing sunglasses. They sat at the huge granite topped island, and drank their coffee.

"Do you girls need a cab or do you have your cars here?" he asked.

"We have a car, but I was going to stay until Victoria wakes up," said Sophia.

"Look girls, you might as well go because I can tell you these people in this house won't be waking up for hours. They sleep all day."

"I told you Soph," said Paula.

"Shut up," she scolded, hoping Paula would not embarrass her with her insane theory.

"Told her what?" asked Jonathan.

"That Victoria's a vampire," she joked. Sophia just glared at her for saying something so stupid and was surprised that Jonathan showed no reaction. Most people would have laughed at that statement, but he just stared for a moment and then walked over to the sink and dumped his coffee.

"Anyway ladies, you can leave when you finish your coffee. Trust me when I say, you do not want to be here when they all wake up." They could sense the tension in his voice, so they decided it was not worth arguing over and left after finishing their coffee.

Chapter 9

Victoria was disappointed when she awoke, hoping to find Sophia still in her arms. She figured Jonathan would have pushed her out the door this morning. She smiled as she stretched across the bed. She closed her eyes and held the blankets close to her face, taking in Sophia's scent but her bliss was interrupted by a knock on the door.

"Come in," she said. Jacoby swung open the doors and came barreling in. He ran across the room and jumped on the bed, gathering Victoria up in his arms.

"Good evening sis," he said. "How'd you sleep?"

"Wonderfully," she said smiling.

"Are you smiling? That can't be. Has hell frozen over? I don't think I've seen you smile since...let me think...I don't think I've seen you smile ever. Must be some good snatch on that human. Does her pussy taste as good as her blood?" he said.

"Do not talk about her like that," Victoria scolded pulling away from him.

"Touchy," he said. She remained silent and they stared at each other for a long moment. "She isn't just a plaything is she? Tsk, tsk sis. What would mother say?"

"Quiet Jacoby. And leave mother out of this," she said as she sat up on the end of the bed. He stood up in front of her and kept interrogating.

"Are you going to turn her?" he asked.

"No, I cannot do that to her. Besides, I am afraid she will leave if she finds out what I am."

"Well, then you have to get rid of her. You can't keep this up for very long." She knew he was right but could not bring herself to finish it.

"I cannot get rid of her," she said.

"I can get rid of her for you." Anger overcame her and she stood face to face with him.

"You will not touch her," she commanded. He had never seen Victoria act like this over a human. Realizing he was in dangerous territory, he changed his tone.

"You're in love with her." She wanted to argue but found it futile. He was right and she could not and did not want to hide it any longer. She sat down on the bed and he sat beside her and put his arm around her.

"What are you going to do?" he asked. She buried her head in his strong chest and let him hold her.

"I don't know."

Word spread throughout the clan fast and everyone knew that Sophia was to be protected. She began to spend more time there so everyone always had to be on their guard. Victoria tried to spend some nights at Sophia's so the house could be relaxed, but always had to race away in the morning before Sophia awoke and she loved lying in bed with Sophia, just talking and holding each other. It made her feel normal. She could not sleep peacefully in Sophia's bedroom even though the room was dark; she knew it was not safe. She knew it would be impossible to always be prepared for the morning sun and she was not fond of injecting herself. The solution always made her sick. It was getting more difficult to keep her secret from Sophia as they spent more time together and she wondered what would happen if she knew the truth. Maybe she would not care; she loved vampire movies and was always making Victoria watch them with her. She could see Sophia's fascination with them but she might think differently if she saw Victoria rip out someone's throat with her mouth. Reality is always more horrible than anything these movie makers could come up with. She knew eventually she had to make a decision about whether or not to tell her but still could not bring herself to do it. The fear of losing her was far greater than the agony of hiding her secret.

The house had been pretty patient with keeping Victoria's secret from Sophia, but they were getting restless. Every day was more difficult as time went on and they resented the fact that they had to feel trapped in their own house. Eventually they started to rebel. Some left the house altogether while others just tried to make Victoria come to her senses. It started with subtle hints, and then threats. When Victoria refused to back down, they started doing things to anger her like leaving dead bodies scattered throughout the house and treating Sophia with some hostility. They knew Victoria would not stand for this and hoped she would come around. It was not that they did not like Sophia, many were fond of her, they just did not like hiding in the one place they felt safe. Victoria realized it was not fair to the others and knew she had to do something before someone told Sophia, but she needed some time to figure out what to do.

She summoned Jacoby and told him she was taking a holiday and wanted him to stay her while she was gone and keep an eye on things for her. She did not need him to run the club, as Jonathan and Derek could handle that just fine, she just would feel better with family here, even if it was Jacoby.

"Where you going?" he asked.

"Europe," she replied.

"You going to see mother?"

"I was not planning on it; I do not really want to deal with her opinions right now."

"Are you taking Sophia with you?" he asked.

"I probably should not."

"But you are," he said knowingly.

"If she will come."

"Like there's any doubt. That girl would follow you anywhere. Have you figured out what you're gonna do with her?"

"No...I can't let her go Jacoby," said Victoria.

"You know you can solve all of this if you would just turn her," he suggested.

"I cannot do that to her. She is too pure to put this curse on her."

"Maybe you should leave that decision up to her," he said. "You know, not all of us think of this as a curse and we don't like hearing this self-loathing bullshit about who we are. We are what we are and you need to deal with that. Embrace it like the rest of us have. We have a special gift and there are many out there who would kill to be what we are and even after over a hundred years you still can't accept what you are." He grabbed her gently by the shoulders and looked at her. "How can you expect anyone else to accept who you are if you don't?" She hated when he was right. Suddenly the room seemed to be closing in on her and she could not breathe.

"I have to go," she said and ran out.

Victoria was waiting on Sophia's doorstep when she came home from work that evening. Sophia was excited to see her but worried when she saw the sullen look on Victoria's face. She sat next to her on the step.

"What's wrong?" asked Sophia.

"I need to go away," she said, not looking up at her.

"When?" asked Sophia.

"I am leaving this weekend."

"Where are you going and for how long?" Sophia was getting nervous.

"I am going to Europe. I do not know how long I will be gone, maybe a month."

"Is everything ok?"

"I just need to get away from everything," said Victoria. Sophia was scared that Victoria had grown tired of her.

"Away from me? I thought everything was going good," said Sophia.

"Not away from *you*, Sophia." Sophia pulled Victoria's face towards her.

"Will you look at me? What's going on?" pleaded Sophia. "You're scaring me."

"I want you to come with me," said Victoria. Sophia relaxed as she felt a sudden sense of relief come over her; she thought Victoria was leaving her.

"You could have started with that instead of scaring the hell out of me like that. I thought you were breaking up with me or you were dying or something. Jesus Christ," said Sophia, breathing a sigh of relief.

"It would take a lot to kill me Sophia," chuckled Victoria. She looked lovingly at Sophia, tilted her head, and smiled. "Just being here with you makes me feel better."

"Of course it does," said Sophia as she leaned in and kissed her. They sat together discussing plans for their trip. Now that her job was winding down, Sophia knew she could get some time off of work and she could use it. Working all these hours was not only beginning to wear her down, it was keeping her from Victoria. She asked her what parts of Europe she was planning on visiting.

"Is there somewhere in particular you wanted to go, Sophia?" asked Victoria.

"Well, my grandmother lives in Warsaw and I would love to visit her," replied Sophia. Victoria looked confused. She assumed Sophia was mixed because of her light brown skin but it never occurred to her that she was Polish. How interesting.

"It's my grandmother on my mother's side. I have only met her once, but she sends me letters every so often. I've seen where my father's side comes from, it would be great to see where my mother's side comes from," pleaded Sophia.

"Can you speak it?"

"No. The only time my mother even spoke it in the house was when she was on the phone with my grandmother, which was not very often." Victoria could not say no.

"Then I guess we will have to add Poland to our list." Victoria did not care where they went as long as Sophia was with her.

Chapter 10

By the weekend, they were off to Europe. Sophia was excited as she had never left the country, except to go to Canada. They were going on a tour of Europe, some by sea, some by land, and some by air. She knew Victoria had money, but she never imagined how much. She paid for everything, including getting someone to take care of Sophia's apartment while they were gone. Victoria never did say why she had to get away and it was haunting Sophia, as she could tell it was bothering her. She could feel there was tension at the house and knew it was because of her. Sophia did not press the matter, figuring Victoria would tell her when she was ready. She planned to make the trip as happy as she could for Victoria.

Victoria's mood lightened as they sailed into Dublin. It was nice to be back, she thought. Her change in mood did not go unnoticed by Sophia as they walked the streets, admiring the architecture. They visited many sites, such as the National Museum of Ireland and the National Library. Victoria talked of the many writers that were born here, Yeats, Joyce, Oscar Wilde and, of course, Bram Stoker.

"I thought he was from Transylvania. Isn't that where he got the idea for the book?" asked Sophia.

"Actually, it is said he never had even been to Transylvania, he just studied up on it to use it in his novel. He did spend a lot of time in London though," stated Victoria casually. She spoke of him like she knew him.

"Do you want to go to Transylvania so we can maybe see some vampires, Sophia?" she cajoled her.

"Funny. I know they are just movies Victoria, I just like them."

"What would you do if you met a real vampire?" asked Victoria, genuinely interested.

"That would depend."

"On what?" asked Victoria.

"If they were going to attack me or not." Victoria laughed at Sophia's response.

"Fair enough. Let us say they were not going to attack you. Let us say they were just like you and I and were having a coffee at a café." Victoria continued to paint a picture of a vampire dressed in a suit, sitting at a table by the window, reading the paper by the soft lighting overhead.
Sophia laughed at Victoria.

"For someone who doesn't like vampires, you sure have a clear image of what you think they are."

"I said I did not like vampire movies. I like vampires just fine," Victoria clarified.

They continued to talk of what Sophia would do as they walked through the library. She told Victoria she would have a lot of questions for the vampire should he be willing to talk to her. The basics: can you go in the sun? Are you afraid of crucifixes? Are you afraid of garlic? Can you eat regular food? What's sex like? Can you read my mind? Can you fly? Can you turn into a bat or other animals? Sophia told Victoria of one of her favorite vampire comedies where Leslie Nielsen turns into a bat but still has his human head. Victoria could not help but get caught up in Sophia's laughter as she pictured the scene Sophia had described to her.

"Paula thinks you are a vampire," said Sophia, casually, as they left the museum and entered the brightly lit city street. Victoria almost choked on her own voice.

"What?"

"She was joking when she said it, of course, but sometimes I think she really believes it." Sophia stopped at the edge of the street. "So, where to next? Are there any gay bars in Dublin? I want to get drunk and molest you on a public dance floor in a foreign country. How does that sound?"

"Sounds great," said Victoria.

They headed down to George's street, the big gay area, and Sophia took Victoria's hand as they headed into more comfortable territory. The party was alive and well in the street as it was an especially nice evening. People were hanging about the street, some lingering in the club doorways, smoking, others making out and some just laughing and enjoying themselves. Between the boys in tight clothes, the queens in their heavy makeup and sequined gowns, and the mix of women, some gay and some fag hags, just out for a night of adventure and dancing, it was hard to tell this gay mecca from any other she had been to. It felt like home.

"So, what would you do if you found out I was a vampire?" asked Victoria. *I created a monster*, thought Sophia as they walked the busy city street.

"Why, do you want to suck my blood?" asked Sophia laughing.

"Maybe," said Victoria smiling. Sophia, being over dramatic, grabbed Victoria and swung her around to face her. She leaned into her and exposed her neck to Victoria and said,

"Suck me, Victoria, suck me dry." Victoria, using all her self-control to not sink her teeth into Sophia's exposed jugular, jokingly nibbled her neck and then kissed her. They laughed as they continued down the street.

They bar hopped until they found a club they liked and Sophia was on her third drink when it occurred to her that Victoria was not drinking.

"Don't you want a drink?" she asked.

"I do not drink," Victoria replied.

"How is it possible that we have spent all this time together and I didn't know that?"

"I have no idea. We do not spend much time in clubs though, we spend most of our time in the bedroom," said Victoria.

"That is not such a bad thing, is it?" Sophia wrapped her arms around Victoria.

"That's a wonderful thing," said Victoria and they kissed as they slowly moved to the dance music playing.

They were like newlyweds on the town in Dublin. They walked the streets until the wee hours of the morning, laughing and talking. They stopped off at a few places that looked interesting to get a drink or grab a bite. Another vampire myth, Victoria was happy to dispel with, was that they could not consume food or drink. They could consume it, but their bodies did not digest it, so there was a short window to get to a restroom or a garbage can.

They headed back to the hotel as dawn came near. They stayed in the basement room of an old Irish stone home that had been converted into a bed and breakfast. Sophia, having been up so late, slept well into the afternoon, yet still awoke before Victoria. She spent some time reading on the balcony that overlooked the beautiful city. Bored, and knowing there were still a few hours of daylight left, she went to see if Victoria was awake yet so they could venture out on the town.

The bed was empty when she walked into the room and she could hear hacking coming from the bathroom. She slowly opened the door and found Victoria bent over the toilet dry heaving.

"Are you okay?" she asked, going to her. Then she noticed the hypodermic needle lying next to Victoria on the floor. "What the fuck! Are you shooting up?"

"I'm fine. Please go, I do not want you to see me like this," Victoria pleaded. Sophia did not know what to do or think. "Please, just go." She backed out of the bathroom, closing the door behind her. *A fucking junkie*, thought Sophia. She knew it was too perfect. That was one thing she would not deal with, a junkie. She had an ex-girlfriend who was a junkie and nearly got her killed and she swore she would never go through that again. She grabbed her coat and left.

Sophia walked the streets of Dublin for an hour before she realized she was lost. She ventured into a pub and ordered a drink. So many things raced through her mind. What was she going to do? Just when things were going to the next level, this happens. She should have known better than to let herself get caught up like this.

Victoria emerged from the bathroom to find Sophia gone. She rummaged through her bag anxiously to find her locked box of blood vials and quickly downed a few. After she felt it kick in, she raced out to find Sophia. She tried to listen for her as she searched the streets. She could not read her thoughts but could sense her if Sophia was open to it. She went in every pub and café she passed trying to find her. Suddenly, she could feel her presence. She hurried over two blocks and around a corner, until she could feel her more strongly. She found her in a pub, sitting in the corner by herself, drinking a beer and staring at the television. She sat down across from her, searching for words. Sophia was not sure what to say.

"Are you okay?" was all she could muster at the moment.

"I am now. I did not mean to scare you," said Victoria.

"Tell me the truth. Are you shooting up drugs?" asked Sophia. Victoria looked shocked.

"No, I do not do drugs. I have a condition that sometimes requires medication. The only problem is that it makes me sick for about a half an hour. It gives me the dry heaves and is sometimes quite painful. I did not want to tell you because I knew you would worry about it."

"Is it cancer?" asked Sophia, suddenly feeling like a complete ass.

"It is more like a curse," said Victoria.

"Are you telling me the truth? I won't put up with a junkie," said Sophia.

"I can assure you that I am not a drug user. I do not even like taking this stuff, but sometimes it is necessary," pleaded Victoria. "You can take the syringe and have it tested if you want." She said it, hoping she would not take her up on it.

"What do you have?" asked Sophia.

"It is a skin condition that... how can I explain it... it is like an allergic reaction to sunlight. The medication helps fight the symptoms. Normally, I just avoid bright sunny days, but I knew we would be out and about today and I just wanted to protect myself. Sunscreens help somewhat when it is not that bright out, but today is quite sunny and I was worried it would not be sufficient." Victoria hoped Sophia was buying this. She was not lying about her condition; she just did not give it a name. She knew if Sophia looked it up, she would find a condition called PMLE that is exactly what she was describing.

"Well I guess that explains why your skin is so pale," joked Sophia. Victoria felt a sense of relief. "I'm sorry I called you a junkie and I'm sorry I ran out on you like that. You just freaked me out when you told me to get out of there like that and then I saw that syringe. I should have stayed and made sure you were okay."

"You had every right to freak out. I should have told you but I did not want it to become this thing we had to deal with."

"Is there any other illnesses you don't want to tell me about that we should maybe get out on the table so I can be prepared?" asked Sophia.

"No other illnesses," said Victoria as she looked down at the napkin she had been folding and refolding since she sat down. Sophia took this chance to attempt to get Victoria to open up.

"But there is something you're not telling me. I can feel it. I don't know why but every part of me is telling me there is something you're keeping to yourself." Sophia could tell by the way Victoria was avoiding her gaze that she was right. She leaned in and placed her hands around Victoria's long, slim hands. "I'm not going to press you about it, but I hope you know that you can trust me. I know I freaked out today, but I have a history of dealing with drug users and that's why I'm so sensitive about it. Sometimes I just need time to think and calm down if I'm upset." Sophia was getting impatient with Victoria's avoiding gaze. "Look at me Victoria," she demanded. Victoria looked up at her, revealing her teary bloodshot eyes. She was trying hard to fight back the tears. She tried to talk, but could not find the words. She wanted to tell her, but was afraid. Sophia could see her inner struggle and it tore her up inside. "You are the only one who can decide when you want to tell me but know that I love you and nothing you tell me will change that." Sophia paused for a moment and then said, "Unless of course you're cheating on me, because then I will have to chop you up in little pieces and feed you to the sharks." It took a second for Victoria to realize that Sophia was kidding. She gave a hint of a smile.

"I am definitely not cheating on you," said Victoria.

"Good, now can we get something to eat because I'm starving?" said Sophia as she handed Victoria a menu from the stack on the table.

"Whatever you want," said Victoria, suddenly feeling a lot better.

"I'm gonna remember you said that," said Sophia as she called over the waiter to take their order. The waiter brought Sophia over another beer, wrote down their order and walked in the back to the kitchen. Sophia suddenly broke into laughter for no apparent reason. Victoria asked her what was so funny and she just shook her head.

"Allergic to the sun," said Sophia. "Wait until Paula hears that one." They both laughed, Victoria's not as hearty as Sophia's.

Chapter 11

The next evening they arrived in London. They stayed in Victoria's favorite neighborhood, the Soho district where most of the West End's gay nightlife resided. From the street, the outside of the Soho Hotel reminded Sophia of the Bingham Building in downtown Cleveland that she worked on. Like the Bingham, it was a tall, red brick building with huge, paned windows. As they entered the glass entrance however, Sophia could see the inside was much different. The décor was a mix of modern and classic London with a large, overwhelming animal statue in the lobby. Victoria checked them in and they settled into their large Soho Suite. The room was decorated with light, warm colors and had a separate seating area with a flat screen television. Sophia walked into the beautiful limestone bathroom that had a large walk-in shower. *I definitely want to have sex in there*, she thought as she looked inside. She stepped out onto the terrace and looked out over the beautifully lit London skyline. She still could not believe she was here. This trip never would have been possible on her salary and she could only imagine what it was costing Victoria, although money never seemed to be an issue for her. She decided that since Victoria did not seem concerned about it that she would not worry about it and enjoy herself. Victoria joined her on the balcony, slipping her arms around her waist from behind and hugging her close. They stood quiet for a few moments, taking in the view and enjoying the sounds of the city.

"Thank you," said Sophia.

"For what?" asked Victoria.

"For bringing me here, this is amazing. I never thought I would ever get to do something like this."

"I am glad I could do it for you, Sophia. I only want to see you happy."

"I hope you don't think you had to bring me here to make me happy," said Sophia. She turned to face Victoria and brushed the hair that had fallen over her face. "I'm happy wherever we are, as long as we're together." Victoria did not reply, instead she kissed Sophia softly on the lips and hugged her tightly.

Although wanting to spend the evening in the hotel, Victoria took Sophia out on the town since she had never been to London. They walked the streets of Soho, taking in the sights and sounds of the eclectic neighborhood. This place was definitely more open than Cleveland, as couples of all walks of life cruised the streets hand in hand. They spent time looking in shops between stopping in many of the gay bars that lined the busy streets. It was great for Sophia, being here with someone who knew the city streets so well, as she might never have ventured outside of the main roads on her own. She was amazed at Victoria's vast amount of knowledge about so many places and so much history. As a student, Sophia was never much into American History, but hearing about European history through Victoria's words, seemed fascinating. Victoria was excited to tell Sophia stories of London. Having been here so many times, it had gotten routine, but sharing it with Sophia brought a new appreciation for this place. They walked for hours and by the time they returned to the hotel, Sophia was wiped out.

Sophia fell asleep as soon as her head hit the pillow and Victoria took the opportunity to scour the city for a meal. She left Soho and headed for the East end of London, where she usually had luck. Stalking the streets, it did not take her long to set her sights on a victim. She did not usually take women, but when she passed this raggedy haired woman on the street she knew she had to take her. She was carrying a bag with cleaning products in it and could feel the hate in her before she even touched her. Victoria saw the images of a baby in a bathtub struggling, while the woman held its head under the water. It was a vision of the future and Victoria was glad for her timing, an hour later and the woman may have had a chance to act upon her thoughts.

She followed her down the narrow street, being careful to stay hidden in the shadows. She waited for the right opportunity and grabbed her before she knew what was happening. The woman struggled with Victoria, but was no match for her enormous strength.

She pulled her into an abandoned building and held her tight to a dirty wall by the neck.

"How could you even think of harming an innocent child?" asked Victoria.

"How...could you know...what I was thinking?" the frightened woman asked, her speech impaired by the tightness around her throat.

"I know a lot of things," replied Victoria. "I cannot let you do this." The frightened woman, realizing she was about to die, pleaded with Victoria for her life.

"I promise I won't do anything. I won't hurt her if you just let me go." Tears began to well up in the woman's eyes, as she begged Victoria to let her go. Victoria wanted with all her heart to believe her, not wanting to destroy a fellow female, but she knew she was lying and the welfare of the child was more important to her than this soulless creature and the hunger she felt was making her decision easier.

"I wish I could believe you, but I can also tell when someone is lying," said Victoria. "And I know this isn't the first time." The woman gasped in disbelief. She wondered how this dark woman could know so much about her. The woman tried to scream, but Victoria bit into her flesh before she had the chance. The warm liquid life filled her and for a brief moment the world stood still. She pictured a happy life with Sophia without the secrets and the outside world fighting against them. She focused on the vision of Sophia's eyes as she continued to feed. After draining her of blood and life, she took the woman to the river and dumped her lifeless body in the water. Looking down, she realized she had gotten some blood on her coat, surprising her usually neat and careful self. She did not need the coat, but was only wearing it so she did not look out of place on the cold London streets. She made sure nothing was in the coat that could identify her and dropped it into a burning barrel under a bridge as she walked through the small crowd of homeless people standing around it.

Victoria returned to the hotel close to dawn. She showered, closed the blinds and drew all the heavy draperies and crawled naked into bed next to Sophia and held her close. The sound of Sophia's breathing soothed her and helped her easily drift off to sleep. Sophia awoke shortly after with a smile and pulled Victoria's arms tightly around her as she pressed her back snuggly to Victoria's spooning body. She lied there as long as she could until her full bladder forced her out of bed.

Once out of bed, Sophia decided to shower and go get some coffee. She looked for Victoria's coat to get the hotel key card out of the pocket, but could not find it. She checked Victoria's pants lying on the floor and found it in the back pocket. *Odd*, she thought, *where is her coat?* She put on her coat, left a note for Victoria and left the hotel.

After settling on tea and a muffin and feeling adventurous, she decided to do a little shopping and headed down to Oxford Street. As she went from shop to shop, she picked up a few souvenirs for Paula, Judy and Maritza. She bought Judy a shirt that had Soho on it and Maritza a silver necklace. After she paid for Paula's oversized London sweatshirt, she decided to try to call her since she had not talked to her since she left.

"Hey, what's goin' on?" asked Paula.

"This is awesome. We're in London now and going to Paris from here," said an excited Sophia.

"Must be nice," Paula said sarcastically. "Actually I'm happy for you, you deserve it."

"Thanks. What am I missing?" asked Sophia. "How's Judy doing? Kelly hasn't been around, has she?"

"I don't think Kelly has left that club, I saw her there a couple days ago and she looks terrible," said Paula.

"I would care if she wasn't such an asshole," said Sophia. Then realizing Paula had been back to the club, she asked, "did you hook up with that girl again?"

"Maybe. She's really interesting but there's something weird about her I can't figure out. It's the same weird feeling I get about Victoria, but I don't know why."

"Do you think she's a vampire too?" asked Sophia half laughing and half serious.

"Very funny, don't come crying to me when she sucks you dry in the middle of the night." Sophia decided not to tell Paula about the incident in Dublin because she knew it would just feed into Paula's vampire obsession.

"It's a deal. Well, I'm going to get going because I'm sure I just racked up fifty dollars in roaming charges, I just wanted to check in. I'll call you in a few days and let you know how things are going." The girls said goodbye and Sophia continued shopping.

As she passed a storefront, she saw a beautiful full length black leather coat in the window and felt the sudden urge to buy it for Victoria. She took in the distinct smell of leather as she entered the store. Sophia loved the smell of leather, only second to the smell of sawdust; of course the smell of Victoria would probably have to top the list. She was not five feet in the store when she was approached by a woman in a long black dress and long black hair that went down to her knees. She was striking with her pale skin and two different colored eyes, one green and one black. Looking in her eyes made Sophia feel unsettled.

"Can I help you find something," she said softly in a strong English accent. Chills ran up and down Sophia's spine when she spoke.

"Um, yeah," stuttered Sophia. "I would like to buy a coat like the one in the window, the full length black leather."

"Nice choice, it will look wonderful on you." The woman waved her hand for Sophia to follow her to the rack with the coats. She grabbed a coat Sophia's size and held it up. "Let us try this on."

"It's not for me, it's a gift for my girlfriend so I'll need a different size," said Sophia.

"Disappointing," said the saleswoman as she returned the coat to the rack and grabbed one Victoria's size. Sophia followed her to the register, where the woman rang her up. Sophia paid and as the salesclerk handed the coat to her, the saleswoman said, "I should have known you were taken, I can smell her on you."

"I took a shower today, do I smell?" asked Sophia, confused by the woman's statement.

"It is not an odor you can smell, it is more like an internal scent, something you can sense." Sophia just looked at the crazy woman.

"What do you mean?"

"All I am saying, is be careful, I have been down the road you are on and it does not usually end well," said the woman as she walked Sophia to the door. Sophia did not know what this woman was talking about and found her words disturbing. As she was leaving she noticed a sign in the window offering psychic readings which made her laugh. This confirmed Sophia's conclusion that the woman was a whack job, a hot whack job, but one nonetheless. She said thank you to the woman as she quickly left the store.

Victoria was still sleeping when Sophia returned to the hotel so she ordered room service and watched TV, or telly, as they say in London. She came upon a repeat of one of her favorite shows, *Absolutely Fabulous*, as she flipped through channels. They were running a marathon of the show and before she knew it, several hours had gone by. Sophia could not help laughing aloud as Eddy slid down the stairs on her roller blades, trying desperately to hold on to the handrail.

"What are you laughing at?" said a groggy Victoria, as she awoke to the sounds of Sophia's laughter.

"*Ab Fab*. I love this show and I think it's even better watching it here in London. I didn't wake you, did I sleepy head?" replied Sophia as she got up and walked over to the bed. She sat down on the bed next to Victoria, who still had her eyes closed.

"What time is it?" asked Victoria.

"Two o'clock," said Sophia. "I bought you a present."

"You did?" asked Victoria, finally opening her eyes. Sophia got up and pulled out the coat she bought for Victoria. "I saw it in the store window and just knew I had to get it for you. Do you like it?"

"I love it, Sophia. Thank you." Victoria sat up on the edge of the bed. Sophia came over to her and Victoria wrapped her arms around her waist and held her close.

"I couldn't find your coat this morning, where did you put it?" Victoria had forgotten about that little detail and had to come up with something.

"I took a walk last night and caught it on a fence and tore it. It was beyond fixable so I threw it away."

"Well, then it's a good thing I got this one for you," said Sophia.

"I will take a shower and we can go out if you want," offered Victoria.

"I was thinking, we would stay in for the afternoon. We can go out later.

"You do not have to do that Sophia, I will be fine."

"I don't want you taking that stuff if it's going to make you sick," said Sophia. She then smiled and said, "I'm sure we can figure out a way to occupy our afternoons inside, don't you?" Victoria smiled back.

"I can think of a few ways," she said as she pulled Sophia onto the bed with her. Although wanting to rip her clothes off and ravish her uncontrollably, Victoria tried to keep things slow this time. She wanted to just enjoy this moment and make it last. She kissed Sophia softly, caressing her face with her slender fingers. She raised her head and looked down into her beautiful green eyes. "You are so amazing, I hope you know that."

"Yeah, I know," Sophia replied with a big smile.

"I am serious Sophia. I want you to know how important you are to me."

"I do."

"I hope so. I want you to know that I would never hurt you no matter what happens." Sophia paused before replying. She tried to read what was behind Victoria's eyes.

"What's going to happen? You're kind of freaking me out a little."

"I do not mean to scare you, I just want you to know that I love you with every part of my being." She lowered her lips onto Sophia's and kissed her. Caught up in the moment, Sophia, her fingers intertwined in Victoria's hair pulled her head back.

"Let's get married." The words were out of her mouth before Sophia even realized she was thinking it.

"What?" asked Victoria, taken back by her boldness.

"I know, it sounds pretty u-haulish, but why not?"

"I think the freedom of the London air has gotten to you. You hardly know me."

"I know everything I need to know," said Sophia.

"You do not know everything you need to know."

"Then tell me," Sophia pleaded. Victoria just looked at her with anguish.

"I am not ready," said Victoria, tears in her voice. Sophia realized she had pushed too far. She brushed Victoria's hair from her face and held it in her hands.

"I'm sorry for pushing. Forget I said anything about it. I just want to be with you." She pulled Victoria's face to hers and kissed her hard. She flipped Victoria off of her and rolled on top of her. Victoria forgot about her wanting to take it slow as Sophia quickly disrobed her and made her forget everything as she kissed every inch of her body. Sophia's soft touch took her to another place, suddenly the world seemed right again and she tried to shove her worries deep down as they made love.

Victoria planned a surprise for the next afternoon. She led Sophia down to an empty movie theater inside the hotel. Victoria led her to a seat directly in the middle of the screen. This was her favorite spot in the theater, so you could feel like you were in line with everything. They sat down and a gentleman came over to see if they wanted anything from the snack bar. Sophia ordered a soda and popcorn with no butter and settled back in the seat as the movie began. *Bram Stoker's Dracula* was playing and Sophia wondered if that was what the theater was playing or if Victoria had requested it for her. The lights went down and Sophia's heart starting pounding as the music started. She loved this movie and could never see it enough. They sat close as Sophia got lost in this masterpiece of storytelling. It was amazing to Sophia, that even though she had seen this movie many times, she always saw something new.

From the moment the haunting music began, Victoria's eyes never left the screen as she became enveloped in the story. She did not even realize how much time had lapsed and was disappointed when the credits began rolling. They sat, holding hands, as the lights went up.

"I have to agree with you, it is a very sensual movie." She was quiet for a brief moment. "Do you think it is possible?" asked Victoria as she blankly stared at the names scroll up the screen.

"What's possible?"

"That their love could last, if he did not turn her?" asked Victoria.

"I don't know, I never thought about it," said Sophia. She thought for a moment and then said, "I think that it would be impossible for it to last because she will eventually age and die and he will stay the same. It wouldn't work unless he made her a vampire also, then they could stay the same forever."

"I guess you are right."

"Of course, it would also help if they did not have a group of people trying to keep them apart and trying to kill him," said Sophia sarcastically.

"Yeah, that does pose a problem," said Victoria smiling, agreeing with Sophia's humorous comment. "Let us say that he did not die in the end; the question would be, would she want to live forever?"

"If she really loved him, she would want to be with him forever, even if that meant becoming a vampire. She did not care what he was; only that she loved him. Isn't that what the whole point of their love story is?" reasoned Sophia.

"You make it sound so simple, Sophia," said Victoria.

"Isn't it?"

Chapter 12

They spent a few more days in London and then went on to Paris where they spent most of their time site seeing. Sophia thought the Eiffel Tower was amazing, but was not too crazy about the cuisine. Victoria was not too crazy about the city, having spent a tumultuous time here many years ago, and had only come here so Sophia could see it, so they decided not to stay long. They were sitting on the bed in the hotel, sipping coffee, deciding where to go next. Their original plan was to go to Stockholm, but Sophia wanted to go directly to Italy instead.

"Are you sure you want to go there next? Why don't we go onto Berlin instead and then to Warsaw?" said Victoria.

"What is your problem with Italy, aren't you from there?" asked Sophia.

"Yes, I am from there. I love Italy; I just do not want to see my mother right now."

"We don't have to go see your mother, Victoria. Are you trying to hide me from her?"

"It is more like the other way around. And believe me, it does not matter where we go in Italy, my mother will find me. She has this special knack for it." She looked up from the map and could see Sophia looked disappointed, so she gave in. She thought if they kept to the main cities, they could avoid seeing her mother and therefore avoid a confrontation. "You are very hard to refuse Sophia."

"So don't," said Sophia smiling.

"All right, we can go there next." Sophia smiled and leaned over and kissed her on the cheek.

"Thanks."

Sophia could feel Victoria's tension as soon as they arrived in Venice.

"Look, we don't have to go see your mother, so you can just relax, ok?" assured Sophia.

"That is easier said than done, Sophia."

"Isn't your family from some island off the coast?"

"Yes," answered Victoria.

"Then we won't go to any islands. You can't bring me to Europe and expect me to pass up Italy, can you?" She held Victoria's hands in hers and tried to cheer her up. "Tell you what. We see Venice, then Rome and then we can get out of here. We will stay far away from Elba Island so you won't even be tempted to go home. I want to ride down a canal in a gondola with you in the moonlight. How does that sound?"

"You make everything sound nice, Sophia. Even floating down a river of garbage."

They only stayed a day in Venice and then they were off to Rome. They spent a few days there to take in all the sites, including a tour of the Cinecittà Studios, the second largest movie studio in the world. Sophia had never been to a movie studio lot before and was taken in by the place that housed such classics as *Ben Hur* and *Cleopatra.*

On their last day there they were having an early dinner in a café when Victoria suddenly put up her menu, hiding herself from view.

"It is amazing here, Victoria. I don't understand how you ever left here."

"You will in a minute," mumbled Victoria.

"What did you say?"

"Nothing," she said, hiding her face.

"What's wrong?" asked Sophia.

"Nothing, I think I will order a bottle of wine," lied Victoria. Sophia pushed the menu aside so she could see Victoria's face.

"I know you're lying, what's going on?" Realizing it was inevitable, Victoria confessed.

"I just saw my mother and I just want to apologize ahead of time for anything that might happen or that she might say when she comes in here." Sophia looked out the window but did not see anyone. She saw Victoria's whole body tighten up at the sound of her mother's voice.

"Victoria, I cannot believe you are here in Italy and have not been home," she scolded.

"Molto sono deluso in voi." Sophia studied her mother's face and was in disbelief. How could this woman be her mother, she looked too young. Her bright blue eyes were only accentuated by her light blond hair that cascaded over her smooth pale skin and past her shoulders, making her look like an angel. She either had a good plastic surgeon or something was not right. Her mother seemed unaware of Sophia's presence as she stared at Victoria. It was almost funny for her to see Victoria in this vulnerable state, like a little kid afraid that she was going to be punished.

"Stavamo andando essere sul nostro senso là dopo che andassimo qui. We wanted to see the sites first," Victoria lied again.

"You do not have to lie to me Victoria, but I am disappointed that you were not going to come see me. And making me come out here in the middle of the day to find you." She shook her head and then turned her attention to Sophia, "I assume she is the reason why you are avoiding home." It was more of a statement than a question. Victoria seemed flustered so Sophia took the initiative and outstretched her hand to Victoria's mother.

"Hello, I'm Sophia, it's a pleasure to meet you." Her mother looked Sophia up and down and then reached out and took Sophia's hand in hers. Sophia could feel the coolness of their mother's skin climbing up her arms.

"Buongiorno, I am Isabetta," her mother said in a slow, sexy Italian accent. She let Sophia's hand go, but kept her gaze. "I can see why my daughter is distracted by you Sophia, you are quite intoxicating." Not taking her eyes off of Sophia, she asked Victoria if Sophia knew about them. "Sa?"

"Not yet," said Victoria quietly. Isabetta took a seat between them and looked at Victoria. Sophia wondered what could be so big if her mother knows what she has not told her and her mother knew this was more than a fling if Victoria was planning on telling her. She looked at Sophia.

"Well, Sophia, I guess you are more than just a distraction."

"I sure hope so," said Sophia, not backing down to her mother's apparent need to control the situation. "I have to say, Isabetta, you look quite young to be Victoria's mother."

"Thank you," she replied curtly, putting an end to where she was sure the conversation was going. "I am sure Victoria will tell you the story of our family if and when she is ready." Isabetta was both annoyed and impressed with the Sophia's boldness. She seemed to be very protective of Victoria, which pleased her and the light shining from her soul was comforting. "Are you in love with my daughter?"

"Madre," interjected Victoria. "Arresto, I am not a child." Her mother raised her hand to quiet her and Victoria obeyed. Although irritated by the way she was disregarding Victoria's obvious objections, Sophia thought it was nice the way her mother was so concerned.

"It's okay, Victoria," said Sophia smiling. With her eyes still locked into a battle for control with her mother, she answered, "very much so." The two just stared at each other for a moment, neither wanting to back down. Victoria, finally getting up her nerve, broke the silence.

"So Madre, what brings you here?" she asked.

"A little bird told me you were here and I knew I could not let you leave the country without seeing my beautiful daughter," Isabetta replied.

"A little bird named Jacoby?" asked Victoria, annoyed with him that he would tell their mother when he knew she wanted to be alone with Sophia. It was just like him, every time she opened up to him and thought he had some sense of compassion, he set her straight by doing something to destroy any hope she had for him.

"You know your fratello; he can't keep anything to himself. So, I want to invite you both back to our casa," she said. "I am sure

Sophia would love to see where you came from, would she not?" Sophia answered for them both.

"I would love that," she said, seizing her opportunity to learn something more of Victoria's past. Victoria glared at Sophia, but could not say no to her mother. She knew she was trapped. She would kill Jacoby when they returned home, that bastard could not keep anything to himself.

"Magnifico Madre," said Victoria smiling, trying half-heartedly to show some excitement.

The trip to their home was not an easy one. They first had to travel to Piombino where the port to catch the ferry that would take them to the island was. Such a beautiful town, Sophia hoped they would be able to visit it later in their visit. Although it took an hour, the ferry ride was so beautiful. You could see the island in the distance breaking through the beautiful sea glass. The setting sun lying on the water seemed to create a pathway for us to follow. We saw a returning sea ferry loaded with waving passengers. Victoria just stared blankly as Sophia waved back at them, smiling like a typical tourist. Victoria's mother had gone inside but Sophia wanted to stay outside as to not miss anything. Her excitement was clouded though by her lover's obvious turmoil. Victoria had been quiet since they left the restaurant, making it for a long journey. She nuzzled up to her and kissed her on the cheek, trying to bring her out of her funk. Victoria gave a half-hearted smile.

"C'mon, don't be like this. It's so beautiful here and I can't even enjoy it knowing you're upset," said Sophia.

"I am not upset Sophia. I was just hoping to be alone with you. The last thing I need right now is my mother sticking her nose into our business."

"Well, I hate to tell you this but that's what they do. The faster we get that part over with, the faster we can get on with us. Besides, how could she not approve of me, I'm amazing," she said, trying to make Victoria laugh.

"Yes, you are amazing. But I do not really care if she approves or not. All that matters is us."

"So stop being such a downer and let's enjoy our time together here," urged Sophia. Victoria could not help but smile when she looked at Sophia's face that was so full of excitement. "That's better." Victoria rested her head on Sophia's shoulder as the two looked out onto the never-ending sea and Sophia wrapped both of her arms around her, making Victoria feel safe. They were both so involved with each other, neither noticed Isabetta watching them through the window.

As they approached the island, the once small blot on a map became an entire new world. One end was a landscape of rocks and green hillsides. It was hard to imagine that this serene place was, just around the bend, the bustling Marina where they docked. As they took the drive up the mountain to their home, Sophia could tell Isabetta was irritated. She heard her whisper to Victoria.

"This trip is excruciating. We should have flown."

"You could have gone ahead of us mother if you did not want to take the ferry. I like the ride along the water and I knew Sophia would enjoy it," Victoria replied.

"You know what I mean, Victoria." *What did she mean?* Sophia wondered. *Was she talking about her?* Sophia whispered in Victoria's other ear, making her feel like the thing in between the rock and hard place.

"Is she talking about me? She does realize I can hear her, right?"

"Yes, I know you can hear me Sophia and no, I was not talking about you. I detest this long journey, but Victoria insists on doing things the hard way," replied Isabetta.

"Sometimes the easy way is not always the best way," contested Victoria.

"Why do---?" Isabetta was cut off by the driver.

"This is the end of the road ladies. You're on your own from here." He talked so fast and his accent was so strong that Sophia did not understand what the driver said but got out of the car with

Victoria and her mother. She could see a large castle up ahead at the top of the mountain but it was still a distance away.

"What's going on?"

"We get to walk from here, Sophia," said her mother, clearly irritated.

"Why do you not call for the helicopter mother?"

"Well, Victoria, since we do not get visitors I sold the helicopter." She looked at Victoria with a sarcastic look on her face. "It seemed unnecessary to keep something we did not use." Sophia could not stand the tension between the two and stepped in.

"You know what, it's a beautiful evening and I would love to walk with the two most beautiful women in Italy up this long hill and if I make it without having a heart attack, maybe we can all sit down to a nice dinner and just get all this out on the table."

"Dinner sounds fantastico, don't you think so Victoria?" said Isabetta smiling at Victoria. Victoria ignored her comment and picked up her bag. Sophia threw the strap of her bag over her shoulder, grabbed both their hands and the three headed up the mountain road.

As they approached the boundary walls, Sophia could not believe the site before her. Her amazement at the shear enormity of the walls did not take away her shock at how run down they were. As they entered, the dilapidation was even worse but it did not take away from the magnificence of the castle. The vegetation growing around some of the walls reminded her of the ivy many Americans let grow over their own houses. She could not believe there was an actual drawbridge.

"This is unbelievable," said Sophia.

"You should see the view," said Isabetta. Sophia looked at Victoria with that pleading look and they dropped their bags and walked to the mountainside. Victoria explained on the way how the house was used as a military fort for hundreds of years, which explained its location and barrier walls. Sophia sighed as she looked out over the night sea. She thought it seemed familiar and then she realized it was the place she dreamed about. The green grass and the way the moonlight glowed on the water, she was almost sure she was here before.

"You should see it during the day," said Victoria.

"How could you ever leave here?" asked Sophia.

"Sometimes we leave to follow dreams, sometimes to run away and sometimes because there is nothing here for us."

"That doesn't really answer my question but I'm glad you brought me here." She took Victoria's hand, kissed her on the lips and the two made their way back to the castle.

The inside was just as run down as the outside, but when they descended the back staircase that was hidden behind a wall, it was like they walked into a completely different building. It was a vision of modern sleekness. Unlike Victoria's place, there was nothing warm and inviting about her mother's home. Bright lights reflected off of the stainless steel and white walls and the décor was only broken up by the black accents. It was a remarkable difference from what was above them.

"It's a lot different than upstairs," said Sophia.

"We have an agreement with the government to keep the upper part of the castle as is for the tourists. It is a big part of the islands history, so we leave it alone and they leave us alone." Sophia was unsure how to take some of the things Isabetta said, they all seemed to have a double meaning. She wanted to ask but thought Victoria had enough on her mind without her irritating her mother. Victoria led her away from her mother and showed her around the castle. The way Victoria watched over Sophia did not go unnoticed to Isabetta, who watched as she took Sophia's hand and walked her around the place, telling her its history.

"Oh Victoria, I hope you know what you are doing," Isabetta uttered to herself.

Isabetta had the girls take Victoria's old room which had not been touched since Victoria left home many years ago. In contrast to the rest of the place, her bedroom looked similar to her room in America. It was very Victorian style with lots of wood and color.

Mother and daughter could not be more different from each other. She told Sophia that her mother liked to keep their rooms the same so her children felt welcome whenever they came to visit.

Sophia started unpacking her things and Victoria stopped her.

"Do not get too comfortable, we are not staying long," she said. "And you owe me for agreeing to come here."

"You wouldn't have said no anyway, I just made it easy for you," Sophia said, grabbing Victoria and kissing her. "And besides, those who keep secrets have no room to argue."

"Sophia," started Victoria. Sophia put her finger over her lips and stopped her.

"I know you will tell me when you're ready. I just hope it's soon, because I don't know how much more patience I have left. I don't like secrets, that's what destroys relationships. I don't want that to happen to us, Victoria." Isabetta watched from the hallway as Sophia kissed Victoria tenderly and hugged her closely. As their arms wrapped around each other, Isabetta could not tell whose arms belonged to whom. She had not seen Victoria this happy in many years and feared for her heart. There was only one way for this to work and she knew Victoria would not turn someone she loved again.

Sophia was not sure what time it was when she awoke in the darkened room. There was no clock and as she looked around, she noticed there were no windows. She looked over at Victoria, who was in a deep sleep, her breathing heavy. She threw on some clothes and made her way through the house, hoping to find something to eat in the kitchen, but could only find coffee and a loaf of bread. *Do any of the women in this family cook?*, wondered Sophia. She made some toast and coffee and decided to take a solo tour of the house.

Like Victoria's home, this house had many winding passages and Sophia found herself lost in its maze. Most of the doors she opened were bedrooms; however, she also came across a music room, a few sitting rooms, a couple offices and a huge library, not unlike, but larger than the one in Victoria's home. Instead of large wooden bookcases, however, everything was white and very bright. *I guess you need a lot of light when you live underground,* Sophia thought, and she now understood why Victoria liked the old-fashioned décor. This place felt so sterile, so cold. She entered the library, hoping to find something interesting to occupy her time.

The circular room was located in a front corner of the house. There was a ladder hooked onto the wall that extended up and slid across the walls, allowing you to reach the books that filled the shelves from the floor to the ceiling. When you looked around you, all you could see were books, like the walls were made of them.

Amazing, she thought. There was a desk in the center with a laptop computer, a phone and a ceramic container with pens and pencils in it.

She walked around the room looking at the books. Some of them were so old, the pages were falling apart. Newer books had a shiny, paper cover over them, but none of these had that. Some of them were too old to have a modern cover and the shiny covers had been taken off the newer books, revealing the plain covers.

She climbed the ladder and pushed herself around the room, stopping in front of a shelf full of old hardbacks with gilded lettering on the bindings. They were all books on history and folklore, but one stood out. When Sophia pulled out the pristinely bound book titled, *Wampyr*, she was shocked to see the pages were old and faded. By the condition of the cover she thought it was a newer book. She put it under her arm and climbed down.

There was no copyright or publishing information in the book, so she knew it was very old and she was enthralled as she paged through the book. She could not read it, as it was written in what she assumed was Latin, but she could make out some of it from the illustrations. She paged through the book, studying each picture. Many of them were typical drawings she had seen in other books about vampires: some of the sun melting them, some of vampires sucking blood from someone's neck and stakes through a dead vampire's heart. What she had not seen before was pictures of vampires sitting around a table dining on plates of regular food. She did not think that was part of the myth. She came upon a picture of a vampire having a baby. But the baby did not look like a human, but a monster. Its face was misshapen and it had monster hands with huge claws. The baby was bearing its teeth and howling and the picture on the next page showed the baby being thrown into the fire. Sophia cringed and closed the book.

She left the library and continued on her self-guided tour. She came to a large wooden door with a V carved into it and it creaked as she opened the heavy barrier into a cluttered art studio. *How did she work in here, it was a mess?* thought Sophia. There were several easels with paintings in various stages of progress and canvasses lying about everywhere-some with paint on them, some blank. The rickety old wooden shelves were filled with various jars and cans of paint and half squeezed paint tubes were scattered about the shelves and some were thrown about the floor. The only thing that was not thrown about was her brushes. Although Sophia could see them all over the studio, they were all clean and standing upright in various containers to keep the bristles perfect. As she walked throughout the studio, she came upon an easel with a covered canvass on it. She gasped as she pulled off the ratty, paint covered sheet. She stared back at herself, her painted green eyes piercing through her. It was strange to see herself through Victoria's eyes and was wondering if there was any significance to the inconsistencies in the painting; her skin was much lighter then Sophia's and the nose was slightly different. She never thought of herself as beautiful, but the woman that Victoria painted was stunning. *She must have been up all night painting this*, thought Sophia. She was so amazed at the painting that she did not notice the lack of fresh paint odor in the room. She was brought out of her daze by the sound of Isabetta's voice.

"She's quite talented, is she not?" asked her mother from the doorway. Sophia pulled the sheet back over the painting and turned toward her.

"You must not be a night person like Victoria; she sleeps half the day away."

"It is hard to sleep when someone is roaming through your home," said Isabetta accusingly.

"I'm sorry," said Sophia as she walked towards the door. "I wasn't trying to be nosy, I was just bored." Isabetta held the door for her as she walked out of the studio into the hallway.

"It is okay, I do not sleep much anyway." Isabetta walked her down the hallway, gearing her toward the library. "Do you like to read? We have a wonderful library."

"I do like to read and I've already been to the library. Some interesting reading you have. Do you paint also?

"No, my gift is music," replied Isabetta. "Perhaps I can play something for you later."

"That would be nice." They continued to make small talk as they walked and Sophia did not even notice that Isabetta had led her back to Victoria's room. She stared at Sophia silently, making her uncomfortable. Just when Sophia was going to say something to break the silence, Isabetta spoke up.

"You have a very familiar face Sophia. I believe maybe we have known each other in another life."

"Perhaps," was all Sophia could muster, feeling very entranced in Isabetta's gaze. Suddenly Isabetta broke the spell and spoke like she had not even said those words.

"I am going to go to the market, is there anything special you would like?" asked Isabetta. Sophia said no and Isabetta left her at the door. She never saw Isabetta leave the house, but when she made her way to the kitchen a couple hours later, the cupboards were full of fresh food. The house was still asleep so Sophia made herself some lunch and headed to the library where she spent the rest of the afternoon perusing the vast amount of books.

She headed back to their room as night approached to see if Victoria was awake. She heard the shower running and stepped into the bathroom.

"I'm glad you're finally awake," she said loudly so Victoria could hear her.

"I thought we could go into town and I could show you some of the island. We could-" Victoria stopped as Sophia stepped into the shower with her. "What are you doing?" Sophia found it amusing how nervous Victoria was at having in there with her.

"I like this side of you, it's cute," said Sophia, teasing her.

"My mother could come in here any minute, she is not big on knocking," said Victoria.

"Isn't it amazing how a mother can turn even the strongest, most self-assured person into a four year-old in a matter of seconds?" said Sophia as she pressed closer to Victoria.

"I am glad you are enjoying this," said Victoria.

"Very much so," said Sophia as she slid her hand between Victoria's legs. Victoria grabbed Sophia's hand and stopped her.

"Can we please just shower?" pleaded Victoria. Sophia laughed, but agreed.

Victoria finished dressing first and when Sophia entered the night air she found Victoria dressed in black from head to toe, straddling a sleek black dirt bike. Her soft, feminine features offset the butch leather biker jacket and the shit-kicker boots she had on and Sophia could feel her excitement mount between her legs. She stood for a moment, taking in the vision before her. Victoria was completely unaware of how sexy she was, which only added to her allure. Her heart pounding, she approached Victoria.

"You don't know how bad I want to fuck you right now," said Sophia as she climbed on the back of the bike. Victoria laughed as Sophia wrapped her arms tightly around her waist.

"I figured you would like this a lot better than walking," said Victoria.

"You would be correct." Sophia leaned into Victoria, blocking herself from the wind as they raced off down the mountain.

They held hands as they walked the narrow streets of Portoferraio, something they never did in Cleveland.

"It is a little more liberated here. Gay marriage is even legal here," explained Victoria.

"Are you trying to torment me?" asked Sophia, laughing as she said it. She was clearly joking but she could not tell if Victoria was when she answered her.

"After this visit Sophia, you might not want to ever marry me." She did not reply as the two continued on towards the marina.

They visited many of the shops along the way and ended their evening at one of the small beaches. As they sat on the beach with a small fire burning before them, Victoria slipped something out of her pocket.

"I got something for you," she said as she slipped a gold necklace around Sophia's neck. At the end was a beautiful green crystal that matched the color of her eyes. Sophia took the crystal in her fingers and fondled it. She felt the smooth edges and got lost in the glamour of it.

"It's beautiful. What is it?"

"Well, its technical name is polychrome elbaite, but I like to call it the eye of Sophia." Sophia just smiled at her corny remark. "It is actually one of hundreds of minerals on the island. That is what the island is known for. That is what my grandfather used to do, how he made most of his money, was mining these minerals. We actually have a whole room full of them at home."

"I would love to see them."

"Then you shall," said Victoria smiling.

"Thank you…for everything."

"No, thank you Sophia."

"For what?"

"For giving me life again."

When they returned to the castle and entered the main foyer, Sophia suddenly remembered the painting.

"You must have been up late last night painting," said Sophia as she rubbed the crystal between her fingers. She could not keep from doing that, it felt so good to her.

"I did not paint last night. I have not painted since..." she paused, trying to remember the last time she was here. "Well, it has been awhile since I have been here."

"Well, you have been here since we've been together, I know that," said Sophia. Victoria was sure she had not been here since she met Sophia.

"I do not know why you think that, because I can assure you I have not been her for a few years, Sophia." Sophia stopped and looked at her. Victoria was not sure what this conversation was about and did not want to ask. Sophia grabbed her hand and led her downstairs into the castle, through the shiny maze and to the studio, where she walked her over to the covered painting.

"Then how do you explain this?" asked Sophia as she pulled off the sheet. Victoria stared at the painting, unable to speak. Sometimes she would get lost in this painting frenzy and at the end would look around to see half a dozen paintings surrounding her and not remember painting any of them. She walked over to the painting and placed her hand on it. She did remember painting this one, but it was many years ago. Flashes of memory were flooding her mind as she traced the lines of the painting with her fingertips. She was not sure how to explain it to Sophia because she did not understand it herself. Although the skin color was a bit lighter and there were some other variances, the similarity was uncanny and she had not met Sophia when she painted this.

"Well?" asked Sophia, bringing her out of her fog.

"I cannot explain it," she said, staring wearily at the painting.

"You're telling me this was painted before you knew me?" Sophia could not hide her surprise.

"Yes." Victoria was talking like she was in a dreamy state and could not stop staring at the painting. What did this mean? "Maybe the universe was telling me that we were meant to be together. Forever." Sophia thought all that psychic bullshit was just that, bullshit, but it was a nice sentiment. She came behind Victoria and wrapped her arms around her.

"Well, I don't buy all this psychic, universe knows all crap, but does that mean you'll stop fighting me now?" asked Sophia. Victoria turned to face her with an anxious look in her eyes.

"I have to tell you something Sophia." Victoria said as she looked into Sophia's eyes, "I want to tell you everything."

"Tell me later," said Sophia and kissed her. Victoria swept her up in her arms, as all her inhibitions disappeared, and the two made love on the studio floor.

Chapter 13

They fled her mother's home that night at Victoria's request. Still swept up in this Euphoria that Victoria had created for her, she did not argue. Victoria knew her mother had to have realized Sophia's uncanny similarity to the painting and would start asking questions and she was not sure what all this meant herself. They decided to head on to Warsaw, Poland as Victoria had promised. Sophia had relatives there, so her cousin had made arrangements for her to stay at her grandmother's house. They lived in a beautiful cottage on a big plot of land along the countryside. Seeing this beautiful place made her understand how many people stayed here, even during wartime.

When her grandmother opened the door, she swore she was looking at an older version of her mother. She was a short woman with skinny legs, a small paunchy belly, scrawny fingers and short, curly, permed hair. *Is this what I'm going to look like?* wondered Sophia as she looked at the old woman. She hoped the good black skin she inherited from her grandmother on her father's side of the family would keep her from looking like an old Polish woman. Her grandmother welcomed them both with big hugs and many kisses.

"Dzień dobry. Witamy," said her grandmother happily as she ushered them in the door.

"Miło mi Ciebie poznać," said Victoria to her grandmother. Sophia looked at her in disbelief.

"You speak Polish?" she asked.

"A little," she said. Sophia's grandmother went over to her and grabbed her face in her hands.

"Sophia, you look so much like your great, great, great, great grandmother, especially those eyes. Piękna. Beautiful." she said with a strong Polish accent.

"You speak pretty good English, grandma," said Sophia.

"I spent many years in the states. I have your mother and uncle there and then me and grandpa come back after she got married," she said. It was no secret to Sophia that her grandfather, now deceased, was no fan of her father's. Her mother had told her that he disowned her for marrying a black man and moved him and Grandma back to Poland. Her mother and Grandma kept in touch through letters and secret phone calls but they never saw each other again, since after her parent's wedding.

"Usiądź, Usiądź, can I get you something?" Sophia did not understand what she said, but understood her motioning for them to sit down. They both nodded no and sat on the sofa. Sophia did not remember much of her grandma, as she had only met her once, at her mother's funeral. To her, her grandma was just some lady in a far off land, not the sweet lady before her. Everything about her, including her cozy house, emitted warmth and welcomeness and she wished she had not missed out on so many years of being involved in her life.

"Grandma, this is my girlfriend, Victoria." Victoria held out her hand towards Sophia's grandmother, who took it in her hands.

"Where did you learn Polish?" asked Grandma.

"Yeah," said Sophia, "where did you learn Polish?" Victoria did not answer right away, leading her grandmother to draw her own conclusion.

"It must have been love, that and business is the only reason someone learns Polish, it is very difficult." They both knew she was right by the look on Victoria's face, and from her silence. Grandma, beginning to understand, asked, "You are girlfriends or 'girlfriends'?" She put more stress on the latter word, acknowledging the difference. They did not know how to answer. She laughed. "I am old, not stupid. It is obvious, the way you look at each other. It's no big deal, we have geje here too." A sense of relief filled Sophia, as she was worried she was going to have to hide their relationship. "Unlike your Grandpa, I understand that you can't choose who you love." She hugged them both again and told them to follow her upstairs. "Come, I will get you settled in Tadeusz's room." Tadeusz was one of Sophia's cousins that she had never met.

"We don't want to put anyone out Grandma, we can stay in a hotel," said Sophia as they followed her with her bags to the second floor.

"Nie, he's at university. He only comes when he's out of money. If he comes, he can sleep on the sofa." The girls just laughed as they continued up the stairs and into Tadeusz' bedroom.

"You girls get settled, I will cook something to eat," she said as she left the room.

"I love your grandmother," said Victoria.

"She's awesome. That mothering gene must have skipped a generation because my mother wasn't like that at all." The girls unpacked and went down to a feast of pierogis, stuffed cabbage, mashed potatoes with homemade gravy and various pastries. Sophia, who had not had good Polish food in quite a while, gorged herself while Victoria ate small amounts.

"You don't like it?" asked Grandma.

"No, it is very good, I just do not eat much," she explained.

"You are too skinny, both of you. We will fix that." The girls just looked at other, knowing she would do just that if they stayed there too long.

"Where is Grandma Helena?" asked Sophia about her great, great grandmother.

"I had to put her in a home, it was too much for my old bones, plus she was driving me crazy," she said. The girls just laughed as she went on. "She has that old peoples disease, you know, Alzheimer's. One minute she is fine, next minute she is wariat and thinks its 1923 and can't remember who anyone is. She was always yelling at me. She can drive the people at the home crazy, that's what we pay them for. We will go visit her in a few days, she won't know you but we go anyway."

Over the next couple days the girls spent much of their time site seeing with several of Sophia's relatives. Besides her friends, Sophia did not really have any family back in the States and she enjoyed hearing the stories and feeling so welcomed, it was something she had never experienced before. Her father died when she was young and besides her grandparents, who were both dead, she did not really have any family left on his side. She was amazed at the way her family accepted her and Victoria in their homes and lives with such open arms and mindedness and they were so giving with their time to show them around.

They walked and rode through the streets of Warsaw, Sophia amazed at all the beautiful architecture such as the Wilanów Palace. Her cousin Tadeusz was excited to show them around the University of Warsaw, where he was attending school. Her cousin Genevieve told her a lot about the history of Warsaw, including how the town was destroyed after WWII and had to be rebuilt. Much effort was made to keep the new construction in tradition with the old. Genevieve took them to one of her favorite dance clubs, The Ground Zero Club, which was an air-raid shelter during the war and they also did some dancing at one of the gay clubs in town, Utopia.

Victoria's favorite stop was the Carroll Porczyński Collection Museum, where she got to see many of her favorites, including Renoir and Van Gogh. Sophia enjoyed walking through the

Warsaw Old Town quarter, another area that was rebuilt after the war. Sophia was fascinated with the Royal Castle and the Market Square which held in its center, a magnificent bronze sculpture of a mermaid. The symbol of Warsaw, *The Warsaw Mermaid* had been in the square since 1855.

It was so beautiful here that part of her never wanted to leave and the other part could not wait to go so she could be alone again with Victoria.

Thursday, after dinner, the three set out to the home to see Grandma Helena. Although the building may have looked beautiful on the outside, it was a typical nursing home on the inside. The décor was old fashioned and the distinct smell of death hit you in the face when you walked into the dismal establishment. There were several elderly people slowly rolling down the halls and one woman was just sitting in her wheelchair in the middle of the hall babbling to anyone who would listen. They could hear loud moaning coming from one of the rooms and a nurse told the resident to be quiet as she walked past the room.

Victoria and Sophia tried to keep their composure as neither of them had ever stepped foot in this type of place before. Victoria was wondering why she had never thought of coming to a place like this to feed. She could do many of these people a favor by putting them out of their misery and no one would think twice about finding their lifeless bodies in the morning. Sophia, on the other hand, was horrified at the thought of ending up like this.

"If I ever get like this, kill me," she said to Victoria as they approached her great grandmother's room. Victoria just smiled. Grandma Adelina stopped them outside Grandma Helena's door before they went in to the room.

"Remember, sometimes she forgets so if she thinks you are someone else just go with it. It is much easier that way." They entered the room but Grandma Helena was not there. "She must still be at dinner, I will go find her." The girls looked around the small room. Besides the hospital bed, the only furniture was a small dresser and a few chairs and family pictures covered the walls. Victoria stopped cold as she was looking at all the photos and took one of the pictures off the wall. There were three women in the picture and one of them looked alot like Sophia.

"Zosią," said Victoria as she ran her hand over the photo.

"What?" asked Sophia, not sure of what Victoria said. Her grandmother entered the room at that moment and looked over Victoria's shoulder at the photo.

"That is Grandma Helena, her mother Adelina, who I am named after and her mother, Zosią, who you are named after Sophia. You look very much like her." Sophia looked at the photo that Victoria had tightly gripped in her hands.

"I do look like her. Do you think so, Victoria?"

"Yes," said Victoria quietly, as the mystery of her love for Sophia came unwound around her. It all began to make sense to her now; the uncanny attraction to her, the deep feeling that she knew her before she even met her and the deep seeded love. Zosią was her only other true love; the love that was taken away from her so many years ago. Somehow fate had returned her to Victoria.

The spell was broken when the nurse's aide wheeled Grandma Helena in. She was yelling at the poor girl something Sophia could not understand and the girl just patted her shoulder, spoke softly to her and left the room. Grandmas Adelina and Helena bickered back and forth in Polish and then she introduced us. Sophia gave her a kiss and said hello to the angry old woman who was muttering something she could not understand. Sophia just smiled and backed away. She tapped Victoria on the arm, who was still turned towards the wall, clutching the photograph. Grandma Helena sucked in her breath when Victoria turned around. At first, Sophia thought it was her beauty and then quickly realized it was fear in her eyes. Victoria sensed the woman's fear and stayed put and suddenly, Grandma let out a deep breath and with a bellow, shouted as she pointed at Victoria,

"DIABEŁ, DIABEŁ, DIABEŁ." Sophia did not understand her, but Victoria began to shake uncontrollably and back away until she ran into the wall. Grandma Helena continued yelling something else Sophia could not understand. "One zabiła moją babcię!" Victoria ran past all of them and fled from the room, still clutching the photograph. Sophia stood stunned as Grandma Adelina yelled at Grandma Helena to be quiet.

"Cicho!" Grandma Helena went over and tried to calm her down. Grandma Helena, ignoring her granddaughter's demand to be quiet, kept on yelling.

"One zabiła moją babcię!"

"Nonsens. Uspokój się," Grandma Adelina said as she tried to calm the old woman down.

"What is she saying?" asked Sophia anxiously.

"Nonsens, Sophia. She is a crazy old woman. Go after her, Sophia. Tell her Grandma is speaking nonsense," said Grandma as she helped Grandma Helena to bed, who was still muttering those words over and over under her breath.

She searched and searched for Victoria but could not find her. Her grandmother came out to help her but after half an hour, they had no luck. They decided to return to the house, Sophia assuring her grandmother that she would turn up.

"She has a tendency to run off when she's upset, Grandma. She'll be back."

Victoria finally stopped running when she found herself surrounded by trees and not knowing where she was. Her heart was racing and she was beginning to feel drained by all the emotion. She lied down on the ground, staring at the night sky. She knew the old woman, but as a young child; a young child who had seen her grandmother's life taken from her by the woman who was just standing before her. What she did not know was that her grandmother was reborn into a new life, a new undead life. She remembered back to when Zosią first appeared in her life.

It was a warm, still evening when Żosią first came walking into their family's gift shop and into Victoria's heart. She was drawn to her immediately and she knew Zosią felt the same when she returned the next evening by herself. She began coming by every night and the two would talk for hours out in the green fields. It was not long before the two realized this was more than friendship and they became inseparable during those few months. Victoria had to make the first move but Zosią was more than receptive. Although Victoria's attraction to women was no shock to her family, Zosią had to hide it from her family, who she was on an extended summer vacation with. Her son-in-law was a wealthy man who often tried to include her on their many vacations, so the widowed Zosią would not have to be alone. Married at sixteen and widowed at thirty-one, she was used to being alone, but decided to go on this particular trip since she had never seen Italy. And at forty-two years old, she was sure she would probably never get the opportunity again. For once, she was glad she listened to her children.

Victoria, being a young, naïve vampire was not as good about keeping the fact that she was hiding something. It was not long before Zosią became curious about her secret and when asked, Victoria was completely open with her. She was so surprised when Zosią did not run away, but not surprised when she asked to be turned. She knew her family was leaving soon and she did not want to leave Victoria. Victoria refused at first, but then as the days went on and Zosią's departure was coming closer, she gave in to her pleas.

She can still remember the smell of her skin as she tilted her head back, revealing her neck. She can still taste her blood in her mouth and the way it felt as it raced through her. She rubbed her wrist as she remembered slicing it open for Zosią to drink from. She closed her eyes as she could still feel the draining feeling as Zosią sucked the life giving blood from her body. She had never done it before and almost let her go to far before stopping her. They laid there in each other's arms for hours after. They might have died from the sun's rays had Victoria's natural instinct had not woken her in time for them to flee to safety.

She had blocked out many of these memories when Zosią was taken from her, mainly to protect herself emotionally. The memories started filtering back when she saw the photograph. The memory of that night, however, was still lost until she saw those eyes, Grandma Helena's eyes. They were the same eyes of the child she saw staring back at her through the trees when she bit into her grandmother's neck. She locked eyes with the child before little Helena ran away in a frightened frenzy. It took her years to erase that look of terror in the eyes of that small child from her mind.

She remembered how the family would not let the child go to the funeral of her grandmother who had died unexpectedly of natural causes. They said the child was having nightmares and saying a monster had killed her grandmother. They chalked it up to being upset and let it go. It was easier in those days to explain things away, before science and psychology had to get involved. And now, history was alive before the grown child's eyes all these years later and she was repeating the same tale as she yelled at the monster who had taken her grandmother away from her.

The family had left two days after the funeral, so Victoria did not have to wait too long to release her love from her grave and into her new life as a vampire and it did not take long for Zosią to adapt. She never had the guilt from feeding that Victoria had and she loved to walk the night. Her transition was much easier than Victoria's and she relished in her new powers. Their love only grew stronger with each passing day and they had many years together until a jealous 'child' of Zosią's had taken her life and Victoria's heart with it. It was after that, that Victoria had shut down emotionally, until she met Sophia. It was all so clear now.

Her thoughts switched and Victoria sat up quickly when she smelled the warm blood. She sat quietly as she scanned the area, knowing it was close. She sat so still, the ground hog never saw her and she swooped him up quickly and bit into his flesh. She felt revived as the blood filled her. She tossed it aside after draining him and checked her clothes for droplets. The emotions had drained her and she felt better now, as always after a feeding, even if it was an animal. It definitely was not the same as human blood and the taste left something to be desired, but when you are desperate, it will do.

Now, in a clearer state of mind, she realized that she could not hold

back from Sophia any longer. She stood up, brushed herself off and

raced back to the house to find her.

Chapter 14

When they returned to the house, Sophia went out into the dark night to find Victoria. She searched all around the house and grounds with no luck so she went up to bed and lay there, staring blankly at the ceiling for hours. She was unable to sleep without knowing if Victoria was okay or not.

Suddenly she sat up as she felt Victoria's presence near. She put on her shoes and coat and ran out into the cool air to search for her and finally found her sitting by a small lake that sat in the back of her grandmother's property. She slowly made her way over to Victoria and could hear her crying. She sat down next to her and noticed she was still clutching the photograph.

"Don't take whatever she said to heart, the old woman is crazy," said Sophia trying to comfort her, from what she still did not know.

"She is not crazy Sophia, she knows exactly what she is saying," replied Victoria as she wiped her eyes and tried to compose herself.

"What did she say?"

"Are you sure you want to know, Sophia?" asked Victoria without looking at her.

"Yes," said Sophia.

"She called me the devil," said Victoria as she looked at Sophia's face to see her reaction.

"I told you she was crazy," said Sophia, brushing it off. Victoria sat in silence for a moment, looking back at the photograph.

"Your Grandma is right; you look a lot like her, especially the eyes, those deep green eyes. You do not just look like her though; the way you walk, the way you laugh. I cannot believe I did not see it before. I tried for so many years to block it out that I guess I did not want to see it. I just knew I wanted to be with you."

"What are you talking about?" asked Sophia.

"I knew her… Zosią," said Victoria. Sophia was sure she heard her wrong.

"You knew her? Is that what you said?"

"Not only did I know her, I loved her. I loved her like I love you, Sophia." She grabbed Victoria's shoulders and turned her towards her.

"What, you mean like reincarnation or something? I'm beginning to think you're crazy."

"I am not crazy, Sophia, I am dead. Well, I guess you could say I am undead," Victoria sighed relief. "Wow. That feels good to get that off of my chest. I have wanted to tell you that for so long." Sophia did not know whether to laugh or not. At first she thought Victoria was joking, but the look on her face told her otherwise.

Victoria could see that Sophia was confused and tried to clear it up for her. "What I am trying to say is that Paula is not crazy, she is right about me. I am a vampire Sophia and I knew your great, great, great, great grandmother, Zosią." Sophia took her hands from Victoria's shoulders and dropped them to her side.

"Are you fucking with me?"

"No, it is true." Victoria waited for it to sink in to Sophia that she was telling the truth. She could see in Sophia's eyes, her mind reflecting on their time together, all the mystery and unexplained events now becoming clear in her head. They sat quiet for a while and stared out at the lake and then Sophia finally spoke, after what seemed like an eternity to Victoria, as she took the photo from Victoria's hand.

"Let's just say for a moment that what you're telling me is even possible. You're saying that you not only knew her, but you were in love with her?" Victoria just nodded. "Is that why you came after me, because I looked like her?"

"I am not sure; I did not even realize you looked like her until I saw the painting. You see, when she died, a part of me died Sophia and I blocked a lot of those memories out of my mind. I only noticed the resemblance when I saw the painting and it was not until I saw the photograph of her that it all starting coming back to me." Sophia took a moment to respond.

"So, I guess what I need to know is, are you in love with me or the memory of Zosią?"

"Does it have to be one or the other?" asked Victoria, not quite sure herself at that moment. Sophia, not quite sure how to take her answer, stood up and started walking. Victoria caught up to her quickly and stopped her. "Please do not walk away Sophia."

"I just don't know what to believe, Victoria. If you aren't sure how can I be?"

"I am sure Sophia, that I love you. I love you for you and for no other reason. Yes, you are very similar, but there are also many differences. That is why I know in my heart that I love you separately. I cannot explain why we found each other; maybe it was fate, maybe it was Karma or maybe it was just dumb luck, but you cannot tell me what we feel for each other is not real. I know the way I feel when I am next to you is real, the way I feel when I hear your voice is real and the way I feel when we kiss is real. That does not come from memories but from love."

"This is all just so much to take in." Sophia stood silent for a moment, still thinking this was some kind of joke. "All right, if you're really a vampire, where's your fangs?" Victoria was not sure if she really wanted to see them or if she was kidding. She really did not want to make her fangs come out at this moment but could see that Sophia was not buying her story.

"Are you serious?" asked Victoria. Sophia could sense her apprehension, making her want to press it further.

"Don't all vampires have fangs or is that a myth too?" challenged Sophia.

"Yes, we do."

"So, let's see 'em then," coaxed Sophia.

What Sophia did not understand is that her fangs just did not come out at any time; she had to be in a certain emotional state, like that of blood thirst or fear. She decided if this is what Sophia needed to see to believe her, then she would show her. She grabbed Sophia around her waist with one hand and with the other she grabbed the back of her hair and pulled her head back, revealing Sophia's soft neck. Sophia moaned as Victoria kissed her neck with her soft lips. Victoria's fangs grew as she could feel the blood pumping through Sophia and it took all her self-control to stop herself from sinking them into her neck. Slowly, she let go of Sophia's hair and leaned back. She opened her mouth and revealed her long teeth to Sophia. Sophia jumped back, releasing herself from Victoria's hold, when she saw her long white teeth.

"Holy fuck!" Sophia exclaimed in shock. She thought she would be calling Victoria's bluff when she said she wanted to see them and was stunned to be actually looking at those two long fangs. Victoria stood motionless, breathing heavy, trying to calm herself so her fangs would retract. Sophia, amazed at what she had just witnessed moved closer to Victoria. She shied away as Sophia put her hand gently on her face, but Sophia stopped her from turning her head. She placed her fingers on Victoria's lips and she opened them for her so she could feel her fangs. Sophia ran her fingertips over Victoria's sharp, long teeth and with that touch of reality finally accepted what Victoria was telling her.

"Unbelievable," said Sophia who was suddenly turned on. She moved in and stopped herself just before kissing Victoria. She lingered for a moment and then backed away which gave Victoria a chance to turn away. She could not calm herself with Sophia so close, so she closed her eyes and blocked everything out for a moment so her teeth would return to normal. She did not even hear Sophia talking to her until she felt her grab her shoulder.

"Victoria, are you going to answer me?" Victoria turned around, now feeling calm again.

"I am sorry, what did you ask me?"

"Is that it, all of it? Is that the big secret that you've been keeping from me?" asked Sophia.

"That is all of it. I hope you can understand why I was not sure if I could tell you about me. I was afraid you would leave me Sophia, you have to know that was the only reason I did not want to tell you," Victoria pleaded. "I am afraid right now that you will walk away I will never see you again."

"Do you honestly think I want to lose you, Victoria? You have given me a reason to get up every morning and a reason to appreciate every moment of life just knowing I will be spending it with you. I have never let anyone in before you and I have never loved anyone like I love you, but I'm a little freaked out right now. This isn't you telling me you have a kid or something, you're telling me that you are a vampire. This is something out of a movie, not real life. Just because I like watching it on screen doesn't mean I believe in it. I'm a realist. I don't believe in god or monsters or any of that stuff. What you're telling me shakes up my whole belief system, it's making me question everything."

"Well, if it is any consolation, I do not believe in god either," said Victoria lightly, trying to soften the tense moment. "I do not understand how so many people believe in an invisible man in the sky, when we are flesh and blood and they think we are a myth," said Victoria, trying to get a laugh.

"Is that supposed to be funny?" asked Sophia.

"I know humor is not my strong point, but yes."

Sophia looked out over the still water, not knowing what to say. Was this a dream? Was someone going to jump out of the bushes and yell 'you're on candid camera'? So many things made sense now: the daytime sleeping, the club, her mother looking so young, the sun allergy, her reluctance to tell me and all the other little things that flashed so brightly in her mind now.

"How old are you exactly?" asked Sophia.

"I will be 162 years old on my next birthday," said Victoria.

"And your mother, the one I met, how old is she?"

"She's actually not much older than me. She is my actual birth mother; however she was younger in human years than me when she was turned. And in answer to your next question, no, she did not turn me. That is a story for another time." Victoria chose her words carefully and asked Sophia, "I know you probably have a lot of questions and I want to answer each and every one, but is that what you really want to know right now?" Victoria was right, she had many questions but only wanted to ask one right now but was afraid to do so. She was afraid of the answer that she already knew.

"You do not have to ever be afraid of me, Sophia."

"I know that but what happens with us from here? We can't go on like this forever, because unlike you I won't live that long and unlike you I will age and become repulsive to you. There doesn't seem to be a happy ending here."

"You could never repulse me, Sophia," Victoria said lovingly.

It suddenly occurred to Sophia that there was only one other alternative and she was not sure she wanted that. She did not want to live to be sixty, let alone forever. Like Victoria herself had said, forever is a long time and her life would end as she knew it. Of course forever with Victoria might not be so bad; it is not like they would get old. *I wonder if the sex is better?* It was great now, but she could only imagine. She got so caught up in the thoughts of sex that she almost forgot the main part of a vampire's life--the killing. Maybe that was a myth too, like the mirror or the garlic myths. She was afraid to ask and decided not to.

"I don't know if I want to live forever, Victoria."

"I am not asking you to."

"So, then what do we do, just walk away? I don't know if I can do that either," said Sophia.

"I do not want this to end either Sophia, but I do not want to give you this curse because no matter what romantic things you see in your movies, there are things about my life that would give most people nightmares." They sat silent for a moment, not sure where they should go from here, but Victoria knew she did not want to lose her. She turned and took Sophia's hands in hers and looked deep into her eyes and said, "I love you Sophia and if that means that I watch you grow old and eventually have to stand by and watch you perish, as much as it would kill me inside to let you go, it would be worth every moment I get to spend with you." She leaned in and kissed Sophia's face that was now was streaming with tears.

"I don't have to decide right now do I?" asked Sophia as Victoria wiped away her tears.

"You are so young, Sophia, you do not have to decide anything for a long time," said Victoria, just happy to know she was not leaving her. She hugged Sophia close and two embraced under the moonlight.

They walked quietly back up to the house hand in hand. Thinking her grandmother probably did not need to hear the whole vampire story, they decided to tell her that Grandma Helena just freaked Victoria out and that was why she ran and she caught a taxi back to the house. It occurred to Sophia as they walked up to their bedroom that Victoria was gone for a long time when she left the nursing home, but now knowing the truth about her, was afraid to ask where she had run off to because she had a feeling she already knew.

They lay in bed that night just holding each other quietly. As the clock ticked, a thought suddenly occurred to Sophia as she was about to drift off to sleep.

"What else did Grandma Helena say to you?"

"I told you, she called me the devil," said Victoria. Sophia leaned up and looked at her with that knowing look in her eyes.

Victoria knew she was caught in a lie and so she told her what else Grandma Helena said.

"She said I killed her grandmother," Victoria said with a lump in her throat.

"Why would she say that?"

"Because she was there when it happened, hiding in the trees, watching us."

"When what happened?"

"When I turned her," said Victoria, looking at the ceiling and avoiding Sophia's gaze. Sophia did not say anything; she just lay back down, resting her head on Victoria's chest, silently freaking out.

Chapter 15

Not being in any mind set to visit with relatives any longer, Sophia decided she wanted to leave. This trip was not turning out how she planned and she just needed to be on some familiar ground with some familiar faces. Her grandmother was disappointed she was leaving early and hoped it was not because of the things Grandma Helena had said.

"That woman is crazy. Victoria should not let her get to her," said Grandma Adelina as her and Sophia sat at the breakfast table, feasting on the large meal she had prepared. Sophia denied that was the reason but her grandmother knew better, especially since Victoria was not eating breakfast with them.

"That's not why we are going Grandma. Victoria is being called back for work," Sophia tried to assure her.

Later that evening, as they were leaving, Grandma Adelina tried one last time to get them to stay. After a half hour of back and forth, they were finally at the doorstep saying goodbye. She hugged them both tightly and wished them a safe trip. As they were about to walk away, she grabbed Victoria and whispered in her ear.

"Zaopiekuj się moją Sophia."

"Oczywisscie," said Victoria, assuring Grandma Adelina that she would take care of Sophia.

The flight back to the States was a quiet one. Sophia slept most of the trip, when she was not tossing and turning. Her mind would not stop racing with the events of the last few weeks. It seemed unbelievable to her but she could not deny what she saw, Victoria was a vampire and she had to accept the reality, no matter how unreal it seemed. She had to accept it or walk away and she knew she could not do that. It did not even bother her anymore that Victoria had been with Zosią so many years before. She realized it may be the reason they were initially drawn to each other, but knew in her heart that what they had was separate from all of that. What they had together was a love like she had never known and she was not ready to let it go.

They landed back at Cleveland Hopkins Airport, got their bags and flagged down a taxi. The driver helped Victoria put their bags in the trunk. After they had placed them all in the trunk, he closed it and got back in the driver's seat. Victoria opened the door for Sophia who was standing frozen on the sidewalk. She walked over to her and took Sophia's hand.

"Are you okay?" Sophia stood silent for a moment, looking at the taxi. She wanted to come home, but now that she was here she was not ready to go back to the real world yet. She needed time to clear her head and figure out what she was going to do. She looked at Victoria.

"I don't wanna go home."

"You can stay with me, Sophia."

"That didn't work out too well last time…I know they don't want me there," she said, referring to Victoria's 'children'.

"That was before you knew. They just did not like hiding in their own home, it will be different now."

"I'm sorry Victoria, I'm just not ready." Victoria, fearing the answer, asked Sophia,

"Do you want to be alone?"

"No, I don't want to be alone. I am just not ready to go back to reality yet. I'm sorry, I know I dragged you back here."

"We can go to my cabin if you would like," offered Victoria. Sophia did not answer; she just nodded her head and followed Victoria to the cab. Victoria got in after Sophia and told the driver where to go.

It was a long ride and Sophia was surprised when Victoria told the driver to stop on a dark, winding road in the middle of nowhere. It was not until they exited the taxi that she saw an entrance to a gravel driveway. The driver retrieved their bags and left them on the side of the road per Victoria's request. They grabbed their bags and Victoria led them about a hundred feet from the road to a small leveled out section of ground with two olive green Jeep Wranglers sitting there. She grabbed a key that was hidden underneath one of the Jeeps and opened the door, started the vehicle and they loaded the bags in while it warmed up.

"We have to go the rest of the way in the Jeep," said Victoria as she climbed behind the wheel. Sophia did not say anything; she just laid her head back while Victoria drove. It was a long bumpy road that took them the rest of the way there and they were surrounded by trees as they drove deeper and deeper into the woods. Sophia opened the window and stuck her head out into the cool air, looking up at the stars. From her view it looked like the trees were leaning in towards each other, blocking out the night sky. It was beautiful as the moonlight tried to poke its way through the dense forest and at the same time, Sophia felt a sudden sense of fear as the trees seemed to close in around her. She closed the window and shivered.

It was nice to be back, Victoria thought as they pulled up to the cabin. Cabin was an understatement, Sophia thought; it was more like a small castle. The main two-story structure was wood with two circular castle-like sections on each corner that were made of stone with thatch roofs. It had a porch and balcony that wrapped the entire house.

"Nice place," said Sophia as she stepped out of the Jeep.

"Thank you. I like it," said Victoria as she opened up the back door to get their luggage.

"I just hope we don't need help, because we're a bit secluded out here," said Sophia.

"Seclusion is the point. But do not fear, I can have help here very quickly if we need it." Victoria kissed Sophia and handed her a couple of the bags. "I would not let anything happen to you, Sophia."

Sophia looked around the cabin as Victoria took the bags upstairs. It had three bedrooms, three bathrooms and a huge living room area with an enormous fireplace in the center. Sophia had never seen a fireplace go right through the center of the room before; you could enjoy the fire from anywhere in the room. As she looked around the cabin, she noticed one thing that was missing. She went to the kitchen where Victoria was looking through the empty cupboards.

"There's something missing," said Sophia.

"I know, I will have some food brought up in the morning," she said.

"Not food, A TV," said Sophia. "I can't find the TV."

"What do you need a TV for?" Victoria took Sophia in her arms and kissed her.

"What am I supposed to do when you're sleeping the day away? I understand we are on different sleeping schedules but I need something to occupy my time," Sophia replied.

"You could read, or take a walk." Sophia just looked at her like she was kidding. Victoria never thought about how Sophia occupied her time when she was sleeping. Victoria never had a TV in the cabin, it never really interested her. She had plenty to keep her occupied; there was a nice library and Victoria had a small painting studio in the shed out back that she could get lost in for hours, sometimes days. That was the problem with young humans; they did know a life without the television, or technology for that matter. In her eyes, it was one of the worst inventions ever created. She will have to figure out something for Sophia. "Well, I have a computer in the library you can use, but I will try not to sleep the day away so you won't be bored."

"Don't cut your sleep short on account of me," said Sophia. I don't want you to change your life for me, Victoria. If we are going to make this work, we will have to deal with our differences. We'll figure it out."

"I hope so," said Victoria.

The two went upstairs and unpacked. Sophia stepped out onto the balcony as Victoria finished putting things away. When she was done, she joined Sophia out under the midnight sky. Victoria closed her eyes and listened to the sounds of the unusually warm night. Unlike the city, it was so quiet here and every sound echoed through the trees. You could hear the crickets chirping and the sounds of leaves crushing under the small night creatures' feet. It was like a well conducted symphony. This is what she missed living in the city. She would stay here all the time but the loneliness gets to be too much when you seclude yourself for too long. Becoming a vampire did not take away her emotions, it only accentuated them.

For the first time, Sophia could see a calmness come over Victoria and it just made her love her more. As much as this whole vampire thing was still blowing her mind, she was happy that everything was out in the open and they could give themselves to each other completely.

"Wait here," said Sophia. She went into the bedroom and pulled the heavy blankets off of the king sized bed and laid them out on the balcony deck floor. She started to slowly unbutton Victoria's blouse. "I want to make love to you under the stars." She kissed Victoria as she removed her blouse, exposing her pale breasts to the moonlit sky. Victoria felt relieved as she gave herself to Sophia. She kissed her softly and let Sophia lower her to the floor. They lay on the blankets and slowly, tenderly, made love for hours.

"I wish we could stay here forever," said Sophia, her head resting on Victoria's naked chest.

"That could be arranged," Victoria said with a laugh.

"Funny," said Sophia laughing with her and then her tone changed as she asked, "Is that what you want?"

"I would not wish this upon anyone, Sophia."

"What if I wanted it?" asked Sophia, not really sure that she did.

"I do not know if I could do it even then," said Victoria.

"Why?"

"When people are turned they are not always the people they appeared to be as a human. Their true selves are accentuated, faults and all."

"So, you're afraid that I might be someone different?"

"I can tell you are pure of heart, Sophia, what I am afraid of is that you will not feel the same for me," said Victoria.

"That could never happen," assured Sophia, but Victoria was not so sure. After all they had been through, she was not sure she could deal with the rejection if she did not feel the same when she turned her.

When Sophia dozed off to sleep, Victoria picked her up and placed her gently in the bed. She covered her chilled body with the blankets and kissed her gently on the forehead. She went to the kitchen and retrieved a container of warm blood from a hidden compartment and drank it slowly. She waited a few moments, but the blood failed to quench her thirst. She wanted fresh blood. She looked in on Sophia who was sound asleep and went out to the balcony. She closed her eyes and opened her ears and stood there until she heard what she was waiting for.

She opened her eyes and jumped off the balcony. She quickly sprang from the ground and ran into the night, racing through the trees, expertly maneuvering through the forest. She raced up a tree and looked down upon the stream. There he was, feeding upon some poor small creature. She could hear the last cry from the rabbit as the wild dog ripped it to shreds. She watched as he devoured the helpless animal, licking his lips as he scrounged every bit of meat off of the tiny skeleton. Just as he was about to run off, his ears suddenly perked up. He could sense her presence and looked up into the trees, but it was too late. By the time he saw her, she was upon him, devouring him like he had just done to the small creature. She could feel the fresh blood flow through her body. She moaned in ecstasy as her body renewed itself. Of course, she only took his blood; unlike the wild dog, she was not an animal.

Sophia awoke early the next morning to the sound of a vehicle coming up the drive. She came down the stairs and looked out the window to see Jonathan stepping out of the other Jeep. He said hello as he opened the back door and pulled out a huge box and Sophia went out to help him.

"What are you doing here?" asked Sophia as they carried the box into the house. They set it down in the middle of the living room and went out for more boxes.

"Victoria called me early this morning and told me she needed a TV and some food, so here I am." He handed Sophia a DVD box, with some movies stacked on top and he grabbed several bags of groceries. "I didn't know what you liked so I just grabbed all the new releases off the shelf, it should be enough to keep you occupied and if you want some different foods, let me know and I will fetch them for you," he said, seeming annoyed.

"Thanks Jonathan." He just ignored her and walked back into the cabin as she followed. He took off his jacket, revealing his tight t-shirt that accentuated his perfectly chiseled chest. It was bright pink with Dolly Parton's face outlined in sequins on the front. Sophia wanted to say something but sensing his irritation at having to come here, decided against it. He hooked up the electronics as Sophia made him some breakfast. When he was finished he joined her in the kitchen and enjoyed his meal.

"Well, you can cook, I'll give you that," he said. "Too bad it's a waste on Victoria."

"Yeah," said Sophia. She refilled Jonathan's coffee as he finished his last bite and put down his fork.

"How was your trip?" he asked as they drank coffee together.

"Eventful," answered Sophia.

"So, I heard."

"How were things here?"

"Crazy, like always whenever Victoria's gone. That Jacoby is a handful and nothing but a big whore. He had different girls in that place every night and when I say girls, I'm talking about skanky hos. I don't know what rock he was pulling them out from under, but they were nasty. They were trashy, obnoxious, causing fights in the bar. I thought Derek was going to kill him."

"Why do you work for her, Jonathan?" asked Sophia.

"Well, it's never dull and the pay's not bad either. She takes good care of me."

"How did you end up there?"

"You want the short or the long version?" he asked.

"How about the short version?"

"Well, it's not as interesting, but basically she saved my life. If it wasn't for Victoria I would still be living on the street, giving blow jobs for crack. One night, I was getting high outside a club when some good 'ole boys came by and were beatin' the shit out of me. The next thing I knew they were flying through the air and I was floating down the street. Well it seemed like I was floating, but it was Victoria carrying me back to her place. She took me in, got me clean and took care of me and now, I take care of her."

"Do you have a family?"

"If you mean the ones who berated me my whole life for being a sissy and then threw me out on the street when I came out to them, then no, I don't. Victoria and the others are my family now. We take care of each other," he said, smiling.

"I think it's amazing that you have such a positive attitude all the time, how do you do it?" asked Sophia, wishing for half his enthusiasm.

"I wasn't always like this. I struggled for several years, trying to get a grasp on everything and deal with it all and then one day I woke up and heard this beautiful voice saying to me: *'you better get to livin', givin', be willin' and forgiven 'cause all healing has to start with you. Stop whining, pining, get your dreams in line and just shine, design, refine 'til they come true.'* and I can't explain why but it was like someone flicked on this light switch inside me and for the first time I could see. I got up, got myself together and started living again. Now, I have a job I like, I am working on my degree and I have a great family. And whenever I get down or I get frustrated I think, 'what would she do in this situation?' and the answers usually come and if they don't I at least can deal with it better now. She changed my life."

"Victoria's amazing," sighed Sophia.

"Not Victoria, honey. Dolly Parton," he said as he pointed to his shirt.

"What?"

"It was Dolly Parton's voice I heard that day, not Victoria's. I don't ask 'what would Victoria do?' I ask 'what would Dolly do?'" Sophia chuckled.

"Whatever works, I guess," she said. He never failed to surprise her. Just when she thought she had seen all his layers, he presents a new one. That was what she liked about him. "What about Derek?"

"I'm not sure of what his deal is, but I heard his sister was mixed up with Jacoby at one point. I don't know the whole story and he's not really into sharing, but I do know he used to be a cop. I do know he is very loyal to Victoria."

"Why haven't you turned?" she asked.

"Honestly, I've thought about it, but decided the thought of sucking blood from someone wasn't so appealing. Maybe when this beautiful body starts to age, I'll change my mind. I will say one thing for them, they are good in bed," replied Jonathan, closing his eyes while he relived his last sexual conquest of a cute, buff, Asian vampire boy before continuing. "So, what are you going to do?"

"I really don't know. What would Dolly do in this situation, Jonathan?"

"I think she would say 'life's too short to think about right or wrong.'"

"And what do you think?"

"Well, if you want my opinion," he offered, "if you're not going to turn, there's no reason to get involved because it can only end in heartache." Sophia had nothing to say, because she knew he was right. The question was how long could they go on like this. "You seem like a nice girl, Sophia, so let me give you some advice...get out while you can, before you get hurt."

"It's too late for that," said Sophia. He hesitated for a moment and then said,

"Well if that's the case, then *'don't let fear and doubt leave you empty and without.'*" Another Dolly quote, she assumed. He got up from the table and put his dishes in the sink. He decided he had better leave before he talked too much and got himself in trouble with Victoria. She was a nice woman, but a vengeful vampire, and he wanted to stay on her good side. "Look, I gotta go. If you need anything else, call me," he said as he made his way to the door. He turned to face her and got eerily serious. "Just be careful." Not knowing what to say, Sophia stood speechless as Jonathan turned and walked out the door. She just stared at him as he walked to his car. "Thanks for breakfast," he said as got in the Jeep. He started the jeep and Sophia laughed as she watched Jonathan driving off, singing loudly and out of tune to *9 to 5* that was blaring from his stereo.

Chapter 16

After Jonathan left, Sophia decided to take a walk. Although a sunny day, the trees blocked out a lot of the sunlight, making it an especially chilly walk through the woods. After walking for a while she could hear water flowing and followed the sound to a small lake with a beautiful waterfall dumping into it. She sat by the edge of the lake imagining her and Victoria making love under the waterfall in the light of the moon. Without even realizing what she was doing, her hand reached down between her legs and under her panties as she pictured her and Victoria's naked bodies together, under the rushing waters, kissing and touching one another. She moaned quietly as she climaxed and then quickly opened her eyes, suddenly remembering where she was. *It's a good thing it's secluded out here*, she thought as she sat up and composed herself.

She got up and decided to head back but as she started to walk, she realized she was not sure where she was. There were no discernible trails to guide her way and she could no longer see the cabin. She looked around anxiously as everything seemed to look the same in every direction. Deciding she was not getting anywhere standing there, she began to walk, hoping she was going in the right direction. Nothing looked familiar, yet everything seemed to look the same as she tried to regain her bearings.

As she walked past a heavy brush area, she noticed something out of the corner of her eye. At first she thought it was a dog, but as she got closer she realized it was a coyote. Next to it was a small skeleton, which she assumed was of a rabbit or other small animal and there was blood on its mouth and fur, as well as under the cleaned skeleton. She stepped closer to see if it was still breathing, but knew it was not. There was something weird about the whole situation, she thought. How did it die? There would be more blood if another animal or a hunter had killed it. She knelt down and looked closer, trying to find a gunshot wound or tears in its flesh. Not seeing anything apparent, she brushed its fur, revealing two small puncture marks, like those from teeth.

"Fuck," she said as she realized what they were. She pulled her hand back from the corpse and fell hard against a tree. She stared at the dead animal for what seemed like an eternity, trying to rationalize it. She had seen it many times in movies, but it was much different in real life. She had tried to block it out of her mind, the reality of how Victoria survived, but could not block this out for it was now, literally, staring her in the face. She was sure that animals were not her only victims and did not even want to picture that. Unable to look any longer, she got up and wandered through the woods until she finally found the cabin.

Upstairs, Victoria was still asleep. Sophia sat in the chair across the bedroom, hugging her knees to her and staring upon Victoria's naked body. She watched her chest rising and falling with every breath, and her eyes as they seemed to be moving back and forth rapidly beneath her eyelids. It was hard for Sophia to imagine this beautiful, delicate woman killing something, or someone. It was even harder to imagine herself doing the same thing. She wondered if she could accept the reality of it all, now that she had seen it. She sat, breathing heavy, confused and shivering.

It was still light out when Sophia awoke, still on the chair. She wondered how long she had been asleep   . She stretched out her cramped up legs and arose from the chair. She took one more look at Victoria, who seemed restless, and headed downstairs.

After making herself something to eat, she headed into the den, sat down and opened up Victoria's laptop. She clicked opened up the internet to check her email. She had a ton of junk mail and an email from Paula. She answered Paula's, telling her they were still overseas and she was not sure when they would be back or when she would be able to write again. She did not know what to tell her, so she figured that would buy her some time to think of something. Too overwhelmed with the thoughts racing through her head, she decided to play a game of spider solitaire to help relax her and before she knew it, two hours had gone by and it was getting dark outside so she closed the computer. She decided to make a snack and watch some TV to occupy her mind. There had to be a *Law & Order* or *Forensic Files* on one of those channels.

She was so engrossed in the serial killer on TV that she almost did not hear the noises outside. She looked out the window to see Victoria running swiftly into the woods. Sophia ran outside after her but she was already out of sight. She could not tell which direction she ran in but could hear Victoria's angry voice and followed it. She stopped behind a tree when she saw Victoria yelling at Jacoby.

"What have you done Jacoby?" she scathed between clenched teeth.

"Just relax sis," he said, trying to calm her.

"Relax? How could you come here, you know she is here with me?"

"I'm sorry; I didn't have anywhere else to go. I thought I'd be safe here," he pleaded.

"Safe from who? And do not lie to me Jacoby." He was afraid to answer. "I swear Jacoby, if you have brought danger upon this place, there will be retribution. Who is after you?"

"An angry vampire father," came a voice from behind them. They both turned quickly to see their mother approaching, her blond hair flowing in the night wind.

"Mother," they said in unison. Victoria knew it must be bad if she was here. She took Victoria in her arms and hugged her. "You could have at least said goodbye Victoria," she whispered in her ear. Victoria started to say something but her mother stopped her.

"But we have more important things to deal with right now," she said as she looked at Jacoby.

"What, no hug for me?" he said sarcastically. She flew towards him and lifted him off the ground by his neck. Sophia could not believe her eyes; it was like she was watching a movie. She wanted to say something but was frozen with fear, unsure of what was happening. He tried to talk but Isabetta was crushing his throat, making it impossible. Victoria grabbed her mother's arm to stop her from hurting him. He struggled to get free until she finally, reluctantly, dropped him. Their mother composed herself and turned to Victoria.

"Do you know what he did?" she asked Victoria.

"No, he will not tell me." Victoria glared at him as he stood up and brushed himself off. "Just passing through town? I knew it. You cannot go anywhere without bringing trouble with you. What did you do Jacoby?"

"I'm gonna be a daddy," he said trying to make light of the situation.

They all knew this was forbidden. Most babies born from vampires were born monsters and, therefore, they were not to breed in that way. There were the very rare occasions that the babies were born normal, but it was mostly unheard of. There was only one time in a vampire's life that they could bear a child and that was the first time they had intercourse after becoming a vampire. A female will menstruate one last time after being turned. This was the last human part of the female to die and if she was impregnated at this time, she could bear a child. The baby had a good chance of being born normal if the father was a human, but never from a vampire seed.

"It is an abomination Jacoby, how could you do this?" Victoria yelled.

"I didn't know she was a virgin vampire, she sure didn't act like it. If I had known I would have been more careful," he tried to explain.

"Why didn't you take care of it?" Victoria scolded. He put his head down and shrugged his shoulders.

"Because he's a coward, that's why," scathed their mother. "I taught you better than this Jacoby. You have brought shame on this family for the last time."

She started to move towards Jacoby again when they all heard a twig snap. Sophia thought it was loud in her head, but did not think they could hear the branch snap under her foot from where they were, yet they were all staring in her direction. They could not see her, but they knew she was there.

"What was that?" asked their mother. Jacoby feeling a momentary sense of reprieve decided to shift the focus.

"What do *you* think it is, Victoria?" he asked sarcastically, knowing it was Sophia.

"Quiet Jacoby," snapped his mother. Sophia stepped from behind the tree and slowly, nervously, she approached the three and stopped at Victoria's side, unsure of what was going to happen. She looked back and forth between the three, trying to figure out why everyone was so upset about a baby and then she remembered the pictures in the book. The concern on Isabetta's face said it all.

"We have to get out of here before Jacoby's trouble finds us," said Victoria to her mother. Isabetta, looking up at the sky replied,

"It is too late, they are close. We must get back to the cabin before they reach us. This cannot happen out here in the open." Victoria grabbed Sophia's hand and they raced towards the cabin. Sophia swore her feet never hit the ground the entire way back.

They raced into the house and down the basement stairs, a place Sophia had been too afraid to explore alone. What should have been a small basement was an enormous underground fortress that Sophia was sure must extend past the house at least five hundred feet. There were several doors surrounding them that she figured must lead to some kind of underground tunnels. Fear was feeding her adrenaline as she looked around her.

"What's going on?" she asked Victoria.

"There is no time for explanations, they are here," said Isabetta as they all heard the intruders on the porch. They heard a door open and their mother hissed. Victoria grabbed Sophia and ran with her to the other side of the room. She sat her down against the back wall.

"You will not want to watch this," she said and ran back over to join her family. "Watch what?" Sophia barely had the words out before all three of them joined together in the center of the room facing the door in a protective stance, bearing their fangs.

A large, bearded man burst through the door with a young girl following behind. The light reflected off of his bright white fangs and his eyes glowed red with rage as he hissed at Jacoby. The girl's large belly came into view as she stepped out from behind her angry father.

"Hey Jacoby," she said meekly. Still hiding behind his mother, he said,

"Hi Haley. You look great," Jacoby replied meekly.

"This ain't no fucking reunion here!" yelled her father. His voice echoed like thunder in Sophia's ears and she put her hands over them as she tried unsuccessfully to block out the noise. The father looked at Isabetta and Victoria. "Look, I have no beef with you ladies, this is between us and Jacoby." Their mother could feel that his anguish was much stronger than the anger he was showing and she realized he was not here to hurt anyone and suddenly felt sorry for him. His only concern was for his daughter and that she could understand.

"I understand your position, but unfortunately, he is my son and therefore this involves us all. I am sorry he did this to your daughter and he will be punished, but I do have to ask why you did not take care of this sooner, she is about to deliver, is she not?"

"It is time. That's why we are here." He looked at his daughter with compassion and then back at them. He felt defeated and did not know what else to do. "She wouldn't get rid of it. She is under the illusion that the baby will be fine," he said. "What could I do? I couldn't force her," he said sullenly.

"I understand," said their mother. Isabetta relaxed her stance and walked over to the girl. She took Haley's hand and led her over to a chair and helped her sit down.

"Haley, do you have any idea what is going to happen when you deliver?"

"I'm gonna be a momma," she said naively. Isabetta wondered how young sweet Haley could be so unaware. *This is what happens when you shelter your children too much*, thought Isabetta. Their mother took Haley's hands in hers and spoke softly to her.

"Oh, you silly girl, you should have listened to your father. Your baby will not live long enough for you to be a momma to it and you will be lucky if you live through the birth at all." The shock on Haley's face was no match for Sophia's. Sophia felt like she was in the middle of a nightmare. *There is no way this is really happening,* she thought. So *what if he knocked this girl up. Big deal, it happens every day.* She thought she must have heard Isabetta wrong when she said that, then the vampire birth pictures appeared in her mind again.

Everyone froze as the girl suddenly screamed in pain. Sophia had heard mothers in childbirth before and this was so far beyond that, that she thought her head would explode from the sound. It was excruciating. Haley suddenly began flailing and fell to the floor. Her father ran over to help her and Isabetta quickly tore off Haley's undergarments.

"Get a knife!" she yelled to her children. Jacoby was frozen in place like a scared little boy, so Victoria ran to get one and by the time she returned the baby was coming out. Unlike a human birth, the vampire baby does not come out head first. They could see the claws as they protruded from her vagina and pushed their way out and gripped onto Haley's flesh, tearing her torso in half in one swift motion. It happened quickly, but having experienced this before, Isabetta was swift to react. She grabbed Victoria's hand that was clenching tight to the knife and together they plunged the cold hard steel into the screaming monster child's nubile flesh before it had a chance to do any more damage. Once the child went limp and released its hold on Haley, Isabetta pulled the knife out and cut off its head. Haley's father stared down at his sweet child in horror as she bled and watched his grandson's head fall to the floor beside her. Isabetta stood and faced him.

"I'm sorry," was all she could say.

He raised his head and stared at her with tears streaming down his face as his emotions took over. Anger started to well up in him and he lunged at Jacoby, but was stopped by Victoria who had jumped in between the two, protecting her little brother. Haley's father did not hesitate as he swiped his sharp claws against Victoria's neck, splaying her flesh open and she fell to the floor. He stepped over her and almost had his hands on Jacoby when Isabetta plunged the knife deep into his back. Before he could react, she removed the knife and with one swipe of the blade, his head fell off his massive shoulders and rolled to the floor.

Sophia was motionless as she watched the events unfold before her. She looked down on the floor and saw blood flowing from Victoria's still body. The sight of the dark red liquid jolted her back into consciousness and she was suddenly able to move and ran to Victoria's side. She was trying to cover the gaping wound with her hands to stop the blood, but it was everywhere.

"Oh God, Oh God Victoria, don't die." Victoria's eyes were beginning to roll back into her head. Sophia started screaming at the others, "HELP ME STOP THE BLEEDING, PLEASE HELP ME!" Tears were streaming down her face as she watched Victoria slipping away. Suddenly Victoria looked up at her and said, "I love you," and then her eyes rolled back into her head and she stopped moving. Sophia shook her, begging her to wake up. Their mother grabbed Jacoby, waking him from his stupor, and yelled at him. Jacoby looked down, and the sight of his sister lying there, with blood gushing from the thrashed open flesh on her neck and his mother's words finally sunk in.

"Take care of Victoria, she scolded, "I will clean up the rest."

He lifted Victoria up in his arms, ran up the stairs, out the door and into the woods. By the time Sophia caught up with him, he was throwing the last bit of dirt on top of his sister's body. He was crying and muttering to himself as he threw himself down on the ground.

"I'm so sorry Victoria, I'm so sorry. Please forgive me, I'm so sorry." He kept repeating it over and over as he hugged the ground with his soil stained fingers. Not knowing what else to do as she watched him crying over her dead lover, Sophia lay down beside him and wrapped her arms around him. They laid there for a while until his body finally stopped shaking and just when Sophia thought he finally calmed down, he sat up quickly.

"We have to help mother," he said and sprang up. Before she could even ask him about Victoria, he grabbed Sophia's hand and the two ran back to the cabin, where their mother had started a huge fire a few hundred feet from the house. The fire was roaring and she was throwing what was left of the girl's body on the intensely hot flames as they approached her. Sophia still could not believe what was happening. She was still expecting to wake up from this horrible dream, even after she watched Jacoby lift the man's headless body like it was a rag doll and toss it on the fire. She watched quietly as Isabetta handed him the demon child to dispose of. He looked down at it, gently gave it a kiss and tossed it in, on top of its grandfather.

Isabetta tossed the heads on last and they sat and watched until the bodies turned to dust.

They cleaned up the basement and burned the last of the remnants, leaving no evidence of the horrific events that had just unfolded. If she had not witnessed it herself, she would never believe what just happened here. Sophia was still unable to speak as they all stood there staring at the fiery grave. Just when she began to calm down, she suddenly felt eyes upon her and looked up to see Jacoby and his mother staring at her. Fear gripped her as she could feel their eyes burning deep in her soul. They looked at each other and then back at her and their eyes turned black as they began walking towards her and the last thing Sophia saw was their mother's sharp fangs as she said,

"There's only one thing left to take care of."

The small creatures of the forest scattered as the frozen ground around them began to rumble and the moonlight shone brightly through the trees, highlighting the glimmering, trembling snow. Suddenly the earth burst open and Victoria's slim hand broke the surface. First one hand broke free, then two; clawing at the ground, pulling her naked, dirty body from the earth. She sat for a moment on the frozen pile of earth she created as she composed herself. When her mind cleared, she remembered where she was and arose and ran to her cabin. The place had been cleaned up and there was no trace of anything that had happened. She went straight to her blood stash and drank its entire contents, leaving the empty containers scattered across the kitchen table, before heading upstairs and into the shower. Naked and clean, she stood in front of the mirror, checking herself in the reflection. She rubbed her neck where the flesh had been torn open, momentarily reliving the pain. She shuddered. There were no marks on her alabaster skin to allude to her misfortune. She was healed, physically.

She dressed and cleaned up the mess she had created in the kitchen. She knew she should feed first but she had to get back to the city, she could find something along the way. She stopped as she passed the remains of the fire pile, looking for something that would tell her if Sophia was somewhere among the ash, but found nothing. She picked up a pile of gray soot and let it slip through her fingers, hoping for some kind of premonition but none came. Her mind was still foggy and she was finding it difficult to focus. Her jeep was gone so she decided to avoid the road altogether and headed into the woods.

She hurried through the forest and through the open fields and then the empty neighborhood streets. She slowed her pace and tried to listen to the night and it did not take long for her to hear his voice muttering to himself.

"You'll both be sorry." She stopped, turned around and crossed the street. The house was dark, but for a light on in the attic and she half expected the shutters to fall off the run down shack as she approached. As she neared the window she could hear him louder, still muttering the same words in a crazed frenzy. She entered the house and scaled the staircase. The short, balding, scruffy looking man came into view as she quietly entered the room. He was sitting at a desk in the corner, his face to the wall, cleaning and laying out the collection of knives before him. He never even knew she was there until he felt her hands on his throat. She picked him up and turned him to face her, seeing the look of horror on his face before the desk lamp bulb exploded.

"I think you are the one who is going to be sorry," she said and sank her teeth deep into his throat before he could respond. She greedily drank every last drop of blood from his paunchy body. She dropped him back into his chair and stood there, letting the blood circulate through her body, renewing her. Her mind cleared and she could focus again. Now she was ready to find Sophia.

She feared the worst as she ran back out onto the street and through the city. She flew through the streets, making her way to Sophia's apartment. She ran up the stairs and burst through the door, her heart sinking as she looked over Sophia's empty home. There was nothing left, like no one had been there. She opened kitchen drawers, the refrigerator, and rummaged through the furniture, tossing cushions aside looking for anything that might tell her something. She searched the bathroom and then went into the bedroom where she searched the closets and dressers. The bed had been stripped completely, leaving an uncovered mattress and box spring. She saw something sticking out between the mattresses and pulled out the only thing left of Sophia in the apartment, a pink bandanna. She held it to her nose, taking in her scent.

Through the window she could see dawn approaching. *At least they left the blinds*, she thought. She knew she would not make it back to her house in time so she closed the blinds and put the box spring in front of the window to block out any light.

She dreamt of Sophia while she slept, imagining themselves back in her house, lying on her giant bed, holding each other. Something was different however, Sophia's touch was the same, but her skin was cold. There was something different in her eyes, like she was…vacant. She awoke in a panic as her fear took over; she had to find her. She just hoped it was not too late.

She decided to go to Paula, if anyone knew it would be her. The shock on Paula's face as she opened the door and saw Victoria said it all. Paula welcomed her in and Victoria paced the floor as she interrogated her.

"You haven't heard from her at all?" asked Victoria.

"No, I haven't heard from her since you guys left Poland. She emailed me to let me know that you guys were still overseas and that I might not hear from her for a while. She said she would call when she got back. I figured you two were still in Europe." Paula was now very concerned for her friend's well-being. Sophia was not the kind of person that would just go off without telling someone. "What happened?"

"I cannot really explain what happened. We were staying at my cabin in Hocking Hills and I had to leave for a time and when I came back she was gone. I was hoping that she came home," said Victoria.

"You say hoping, like you know something bad might have happened to her," said Paula, her voice getting louder. "I knew something was off about you, what the hell is going on?" Victoria just looked at her and then headed for the door. "Where are you going?"

"I'll let you know if I find her," said Victoria as she ran out the door.

"What do you mean if?" Paula yelled after her, but she was already gone. She just stood there in shock, not sure what to do. She called Maritza, who had not heard from her either, and now she was scared.

Not sure where to look next, Victoria decided to head home. Maybe someone there knew something. Maybe Jacoby was there and could tell her what happened. Derek and Jonathan were inside the club setting up tables when she stormed through the door. Jonathan, excited to see her, ran over and hugged her.

"I am so glad you're back, things have been crazy without you here," he said. She half-hugged him as she looked over at Derek who was looking serious, as always.

"Is Jacoby here?" she asked as he released her.

"No, thank God. That crazy mother fucker flew out of here six weeks ago when some big hairy guy came looking for him and he hasn't been back since. Did you know he knocked up some young thing? Crazy fool."

"Yeah, I know. I thought maybe he would have come back here after it was taken care of." She looked at Derek who remained quiet and kept working. She walked past Jonathan and over to the quiet bouncer, who stopped working when she came up beside him. "I need your help Derek, I cannot find Sophia." He looked at her calmly, showing no emotion. *He is so good at hiding his thoughts*, thought Victoria as she unsuccessfully tried to read him.

"Everything has been taken care of, Victoria, just like your mother requested."

"She was here?"

"Yes. Why don't you go freshen up and everything will become clearer," he said softly. "And stay out of my head." She did not know what to make of his demeanor; he was not usually so quiet, but something told her not to push the issue right now and she walked away. She stopped when she reached the exit door and turned to see them both looking at her, Derek stone faced and Jonathan smiling. She turned and left out the door and down the long hallway to her bedroom, wondering what her mother had done to make them act this way.

She was taken aback by the scene before her when she opened her bedroom doors. The place was filled with glowing candles that reflected off the freshly painted golden walls. New bedding replaced her antique quilts, setting off the ornate carvings on the giant headboard. It was so bright. She wondered if this was part of her mother's instructions or if the boys did this on their own. Well, she knew it was not Jonathan, because then it would be pink. She went over to the bed and stroked the satin comforter.

"I hope you like it," said a familiar voice from behind her. Victoria spun around to see Sophia standing face to face with her. A sense of relief rushed over her and she let out a sigh. It was Sophia, but it was not the same Sophia she knew. There was a distinctive, angelic aura about her. Victoria's heart started pounding as she approached her and placed her hand on Sophia's cold skin.

"Oh, Sophia, I am so sorry about this. I will never forgive myself for letting this happen," said Victoria. "Jacoby will pay for bringing all this mess."

"Well, you didn't turn me, so I guess you're off the hook for that one," said Sophia calmly. "He did not turn me either, but as far as Jacoby's concerned, he is the only reason I'm still here. You're mother had other plans, but he convinced her otherwise."

"I never intended for this to happen. I never wanted you to have this curse."

"I've made my peace with it, Victoria...besides, there's nothing that can change it now. It would have come to this eventually, if we were to stay together. I guess that's no concern anymore" Sophia seemed especially serene. Then something occurred to her. "You know, I thought my heart would have stopped beating though, since I'm dead and all. But I guess something's got to keep the blood moving."

"How do you feel Sophia? Has everything changed?" she asked nervously. Sophia looked deep into her eyes like never before.

"The way I feel about you hasn't changed, if that's what you're worried about. If anything, I feel it stronger now. I feel everything stronger now, it's amazing. It's like the whole world has opened up in a completely new way...I feel incredible." Sophia held out her arms to Victoria who gratefully fell into them, feeling an overwhelming sense of relief. Sophia held her close, stroking her soft dark hair.

"I guess I am stuck with you forever now," said Victoria.

"As you said before my sweet Victoria, forever is a long time."

"Not long enough," said Victoria as she kissed Sophia on her new, vampire lips.

D.M. Glass fell in love with vampires the first time she saw the original Dracula movie. The darkness, the sensualness and those awesome teeth grabbed hold of her and never let go. A native of Cleveland, Ohio, she earned her Bachelor's Degree in Business from Mount Union College and currently works as a carpenter while writing whenever possible. She also writes poetry and humorous non-fiction and recently won honorable mention for her essay Evil Kitty in the Writer's Digest annual completion. She is currently working on a chapbook as well as editing the sequel to Pulse.

http://www.facebook.com/dmglassauthor

Made in the USA
Middletown, DE
27 February 2022

61873775R00130